The greatest problem
done a fabulous job o
Read this book. Use t
dorse this book.

MW01129927

Caris Snider is a friend every teenager wishes they had. In the 90 Day Anxiety Elephants for Teens Devotional she comes alongside as an ally, coach, and fierce example of what happens when Jesus is invited into the process of trampling debilitating anxiety elephants. I will definitely be sharing this powerful, practical, and profound resource with my counseling clients and their parents!

Teens, you are not alone! With the kind of tenderness that comes from someone who has "been there," Caris Snider helps teens apply the truth of God's word to their lives. Young people who embark on this 90 day journey will find Caris to be a wise and judgement-free guide.

Caris Snider provides students and parents a rich resource! This devotional is filled with practical life experiences that everyone will relate to. Her insight into anxiety and her practical understanding of how to reframe and create new patterns of thinking from biblical truth is spot on. I highly recommend this weapon for warring against the Anxiety Elephants.

ANXIETY

ELEPHANTS

FOR TEENS

A 90 DAY DEVOTIONAL

CARIS SNIDER

END GAME
Press

Anxiety Elephants for Teens Devotional

End Game Press books may be purchased in bulk at special discounts for sales promotion, corporate gifts, ministry, fund-raising, or educational purposes. Special editions can also be created to specifications. For details, contact Special Sales Dept., End Game Press, P.O. Box 206, Nesbit, MS 38651 or info@endgamepress.com.

Visit our website at www.endgamepress.com.

Library of Congress Control Number: 2023951933
Hardcover ISBN: 9781637971314
Paperback ISBN: 9781637972076
eBook ISBN: 9781637972083

Cover by Christopher Gilbert, Gilbert & Carlson Design, LLC
Interior Design by Typewriter Creative Co.

Published in association with Del Duduit of the Cyle Young Literary Elite, LLC.

Printed in the United States of America
10 9 8 7 6 5 4 3 2 1

Dedicated to all the teenagers and the guardians raising them.

Parents, never stop praying over their hearts and minds. Teens, know you are loved by God, and He will see you through this mental battle!

CONTENTS

ANXIETY SYMPTOMS

Anxiety can reveal itself through different indicators. With that in mind, I wanted to hear from you—the teens. I did a survey asking teens to share symptoms they notice when Anxiety Elephants come. The top answers are below to bring awareness to the signs others have experienced, so you know you are not alone. You may discover you have felt all these symptoms or only a few. It could be possible what you experience is not even listed here.

Symptoms:

- A constant state of worry
- Shaking or trembling
- Stomachache
- Rapid heartbeat
- Fear
- Loss of sleep
- Fidgeting
- Uncontrollable outbursts of anger or sadness
- Inability to concentrate
- Headache
- Difficulty breathing
- Nausea

For an additional symptoms checklist for anxiety in teens, go to:

https://www.nami.org/About-Mental-Illness/Mental-Health-Conditions/Anxiety-Disorders[1]

CURRENT COPING METHODS

Another question on my survey was asking you about coping mechanisms. Your answers took me back to my days as a teenager and thrust me into the pressure-filled world you live in right now. I remember responding to anxiety in similar ways to those listed below, but not realizing what was truly happening. When I was your age, I experienced anxiousness, but the burden you now bear is beyond fully wrapping my brain around. The constant movement of your thoughts, emotions, and schedules brings many of you to cope with anxiety in the following ways:

- Pressure to fix it alone

- Panic

- Loss of appetite

- The inability to tell anyone

- Isolation

- The mindless scroll of social media

- Denial that anything is going on

You no longer have to hide. What you are going through is real. As you flip through the pages of this devotional, that reality will not be dismissed. An invitation is before you to hear God's word which is trustworthy and true. He is not mad at you for experiencing anxiety. Your Heavenly Father has different strategies to offer in combat against the Anxiety Elephants attacking you.

INTRODUCTION

Heart racing . . . stomach churning . . . knees locked in paralysis. Can you feel it? You are walking into school, getting ready for a first date, squaring up to shoot the ball at the buzzer, or logging into your computer for a test, and here they come—Anxiety Elephants.

You know the feeling, right? They charge out of nowhere waiting for the right moment to strike. At this point, it's too late. There is nothing you can do to stop them. They pounce. A herd of elephants jump up and down on your chest.

If you struggle with what I've described, know you are not alone. I hid my clash with anxiety for a long time. I thought Anxiety Elephants—as I like to call them—only attacked me. I didn't know others faced the same silent battle.

Growing up, I dealt with a lot of anxiety, but I didn't know what it was. My heart would race, and worrisome thoughts plagued me at night. Sometimes trying to get one breath out was exhausting. I will never forget waking up in fifth grade with blurry vision and extreme migraines. I told my parents my symptoms, and they took me to the doctor. He mentioned anxiety, and I was relieved to know what was happening inside my body. However, he didn't offer any solutions. My strategy to cope became a plan of hiding and avoiding. But this inflamed my anxiousness instead of calming it down. My anxiety was almost out-of-control during those middle school and high school years.

I want to give you what I wish someone would have given me to help stomp out Anxiety Elephants. Over the next ninety days, you will find scripture, healthy coping strategies, journaling pages, and an application step to focus on the next small thing to do each day. You will be equipped to overcome Anxiety Elephants one moment at a time.

Anxiety will use repetition to attack. It doesn't use a million different messages to invade your life—the lies are always the same. In the following pages, you will find truth repeated to break the hold of untruths looping in your mind. This will be a process and not an overnight fix as God reveals His grace and truth to your mental stress.

Are you ready? Let's do this together.

ONE

"'My soul is overwhelmed with sorrow to the
point of death,' he said to them."

Mark 14:34a, NIV

The bump in the road jolted orange juice onto my clothes. I couldn't take it anymore. I was done. My brother made it to school before the tardy bell rang, but my feet were glued to the puddle of Vitamin C on the floorboard. I peeled myself off the seat with a whisper. "I am going back home." Between classes, extracurricular activities, and life decisions I was expected to make, an overwhelming flood of anxiety was drowning me from the inside out. My mom met me at the front door with silence and open arms. I crawled back into bed believing I was the only one crumbling under the weight of my anxious thoughts and feelings.

Did Jesus deal with the overwhelm of life? Do we have a Savior who understands what carrying the weight of the world feels like?

Yes.

My mouth hit the floor the first time I read this passage and saw the words Jesus spoke. Knowing our Savior *has* experienced what being overwhelmed feels like? That brought a sigh of relief.

He didn't hide. Jesus made it very clear how He was feeling. He didn't push it down and camouflage the situation with, "I'm good," "I'm fine," or "No worries"!

Jesus told His disciples, James, Peter, and John, to go a little further with Him into the garden. He wanted His friends close in His time of need. Friends can't prevent you from feeling overwhelmed, but they can help you walk through it.

Jesus prayed. He went to His Father and laid it all out. He called God, *Abba*. This word is an Aramaic word meaning "Daddy." Jesus was close to God and knew He could go to Him with what was going on. By doing this, He shows us we can do the same. If you continue reading this passage of scripture, Jesus prayed two more times, leaning closer into His Father's love. It was not a one-and-done prayer. If you find yourself praying the same thing, keep praying.

We see God didn't tell Jesus to suck it up or get back to work. He met Jesus there in that moment. He will do the same for you in the middle of your distress.

THE NEXT SMALL STEP

Follow the example of Jesus and have a transparent
talk with God. He can handle everything you have
buried inside that needs to be shoveled out.

PRAYER

*If Jesus can be honest with you, God, so will I. What
is really going on is . . . (fill in the blank).*

JOURNAL

....

....

....

....

....

....

TWO

"Come to me, all you who are weary and
burdened, and I will give you rest."

Matthew 11:28, NIV

Anxiety Elephants—where in the world do they come from?

At your age, anxiety made it difficult for me to live life. I didn't know
what I was battling had a name. I thought the symptoms I experienced were unique to me and possibly made up in my head. My
heart would beat at an alarming speed. For what felt like hours, the
heaviest feeling I had ever experienced would weigh down my chest
and steal my breath away. The attacks would come at random times
leaving me discouraged and disheartened.

Close your eyes and imagine a herd of elephants charging towards
you as fast as they can. Picture them jumping on top of your chest
like a trampoline, and they just. won't. stop. That is what an anxiety
attack feels like.

From the start, I hid my anxiety behind a smile. Finding relief was
a huge desire of my heart, but admitting I needed it was the biggest
barrier to overcome. What would others think if they knew of my
dark secret? I didn't realize struggling with Anxiety Elephants was a
common thing for teenagers.

Knowing that I could come to Jesus with all my burdens changed
things.

No matter what you do, you may still have moments where the
breath is knocked out of you as Anxiety Elephants kick you into a
cloud of dust and make you feel like you're landing on the hard, cold
ground. I do. But our scripture gives us a powerful reminder. When

you experience these kinds of attacks, Jesus invites you to come and find rest in His supernatural peace.

THE NEXT SMALL STEP

Jesus is inviting you to come. He's giving you the opportunity to freely acknowledge the Anxiety Elephants attacking you. Take this step to pray about the mental intrusion they have caused.

PRAYER

Dear Jesus, thank You for inviting me to come with all my burdens. I am accepting Your appeal to no longer do this on my own.

JOURNAL

....

....

....

....

....

....

....

....

....

....

THREE

"But it is the spirit in a person, the breath of the
Almighty, that gives them understanding."

Job 32:8, NIV

I will never forget the day I sat down on my beige couch and thought it would be the last time I would enjoy its comfort. In a moment, my breathing went from easygoing to hard work.

Breathing is a simple yet powerful part of our survival. We don't think about this function of living until gasping for air leaves us clutching our chest. Anxiety can bring on this dreadful experience.

God spoke the world and universe into existence. We read in the very first chapter of Genesis, "Let there be light," and there was light (verse 3). God did this for the trees, animals, water, and sky. For man, He did something different. Genesis 2:7 tells us, *"Then the Lord God formed a man from the dust of the ground and breathed into his nostrils the breath of life, and the man became a living being."*

It's hard to imagine that the very breath of God is within us.

In our opening verse, young Elihu is reminding Job and his friends that wisdom and understanding are from the breath of the Almighty God. When we pause and breathe in this truth, it shifts us out of panic and into a focused thought process.

By taking deep breaths in through your nose and exhaling out through your mouth, you allow the movement of air through your lungs to switch on the thinking part of your brain. This deviates control from your emotional brain when anxiety wants to take charge.

You don't have to hold your breath anymore waiting for the next attack. Take control of your breathing and let God's breath fill your life.

THE NEXT SMALL STEP

Practice deep breathing. A few times throughout the day, take a deep breath in your nose and slowly exhale out through your mouth. As you work to develop this habit, it will become a natural response when Anxiety Elephants try to take your breath away.

PRAYER

Thank You, God, for breathing Your breath in my lungs.

JOURNAL

....

....

....

....

....

....

....

....

....

....

....

FOUR

"Go now, write it on a tablet for them, inscribe it on a scroll, that for the days to come it may be an everlasting witness."

Isaiah 30:8, NIV

No way. No way am I going to curl up on my bed and write down the happenings of my day in a diary with a unicorn and secret lock tucked away under my pillow. This is what I envisioned when the idea of journaling was presented to me. Writing things down felt dated and out of touch with my current season of life. I couldn't understand how putting things down on paper could be helpful. Surely, there were other options I could use with technology involved.

Then, I tried it one day.

I had an old, college-ruled notebook with a few blank pages left. I opened it and stared at the blue lines encouraging me to give it a chance. At first, words came out in a single file line, revealing awful lies that had taken root in my heart. Eventually, sentences began to flow. Just letting the ink move without worrying about punctuation and correct spelling was freeing. The focus was to get out everything coming to my mind in the moment.

Something was different. Journaling allowed me to feel lighter. It opened my eyes to how much pain I had been carrying around every day. Looking back on those pages now, I realize all the work God has done in my life and the victories that have taken place.

By using the journal section in this devotional, you can look back and see the changes God is making in your life. Writing out the classified pain you have been keeping to yourself stops the Anxiety Elephants from using this hush-hush material against you. You can unapologetically let go of every awful thought and adversity you have faced. Putting the hidden words on paper will unlock holy change in your heart.

THE NEXT SMALL STEP

Just give it a try. This will be between you and the Lord. Start with a list of words if sentences are not forming. It could feel awkward at first, but don't hold back anything wanting to come out.

PRAYER

Help me to try this new thing, God. Give me the freedom to let the words flow.

JOURNAL

....

....

....

....

....

....

....

....

....

....

FIVE

"If any of you lacks wisdom, you should ask
God, who gives generously to all without
finding fault, and it will be given to you."

James 1:5, NIV

All in favor of getting rid of tests, raise your hand! My sixteen-year-old self would have agreed the day I failed my driver's license test. Heart racing, palms sweating, and breath, well, I couldn't breathe. We arrived at the courthouse early that morning. Most count down the days to when they can grab the keys and get behind the wheel. I waited two months to make sure I had practiced enough not to make a mistake. My name was called and my brain went into flight mode. The instructor said turn left. I heard her, but my mind told me to turn right. She yelled. I cried. It was horrible. Mercy was given, and I was allowed to take the test over. I passed, but no one knew I had failed the first time. Except you who are now in on my secret.

I thought I was the only one who struggled with any type of test.

Are tests hard for you? Do you study and prepare, only to find yourself going blank at the sight of the first question? Test anxiety is a very real thing. It can block your brain from thinking clearly and cause emotions to take over, keeping you from answering any questions before the bell rings.

How can you deal with test anxiety? Our scripture tells us to ask God for wisdom. Talking to God about a test is not too small for Him. If the test is important to you, it is important to Him.

Instead of waiting until the night before the test, change your habit and study in small amounts several days in advance. Invite a group of friends over to discuss the material and make sure everyone understands what the teacher will be asking you to do. When test day arrives, take a deep breath. Exhale worry and ask God to give you wisdom. All you can do is your best and trust Him with the rest.

THE NEXT SMALL STEP

Create a plan for your next test. Look at the calendar
and designate time to prepare. If the material is difficult,
who is one friend or teacher you can ask for help?

PRAYER

*Thank you, God, for caring about everything, including my
tests. Give me the wisdom I need and the willingness to try
studying earlier instead of waiting until the last minute.*

JOURNAL

....

....

....

....

....

....

....

....

....

SIX

"That is why, for Christ's sake, I delight in weaknesses,
in insults, in hardships, in persecutions, in difficulties.
For when I am weak, then I am strong."

2 Corinthians 12:10, NIV

Going through the middle school years can be brutal. You try so hard to find your place, to blend in, and to not stick out. As a teenager, the last thing you want to do is show any frail crack in your armor. We think this self-protective mindset starts when the hormones hit, or at least that is what adults say, but that is not always the case. In first grade, a boy in my classroom gathered everyone around to make fun of a physical weakness I was unable to disguise. I was born with a mild form of cerebral palsy, causing the muscles in my left arm to be tightly drawn upward and my foot to be turned inward causing me to walk with a limp. He held his arms up like a rabbit and began to hop around me while saying that is what I looked like.

Pretty harsh, right? When hard things happen to you, they can stick in your heart, forever shaping how you choose to live . . . or hide.

I went home and cried but told no one. This "friend" used my weakness against me. Long before the days of a locker combination entered my life, this idea to always emerge strong, never frail, was formed. I thought that to avoid being made fun of again, I had to be perfect and never show my weaknesses. Do you also put yourself under this constant strain of toughness?

Because I was mistaken. We do not have to hide struggles like anxiety and pretend to have it all together. The truth is none of us *do* have it all together. Being weak is normal, and we can be open and honest about our imperfections with God.

Delighting in your weaknesses will feel awkward at first. The world has trained you to do the opposite and never admit to where you are lacking. In 2 Corinthians, Paul knows God's way will relieve the pressure of needing to be capable on our own. Coming to Him with our weaknesses allows Jesus to prop us up in His strength.

THE NEXT SMALL STEP

Acknowledge your weaknesses. Allow Jesus into those places so His strength can persevere through you.

PRAYER

Dear Lord, help me to remember that being weak is not abnormal...we are all weak. Thank You for the reminder that Your strength will shine through my weakness.

JOURNAL

....

....

....

....

....

....

....

....

....

....

SEVEN

"The Lord himself goes before you and will be
with you; he will never leave you nor forsake you.
Do not be afraid; do not be discouraged."

Deuteronomy 31:8, NIV

The heavy feeling on your chest has snuck back in. All you were trying to do was complete the periodic table assignment, finish your paper, and correct the two questions you missed on the pop quiz in math. Pressure is building up inside. Your breathing has accelerated. The air going in and out has moved from a steady flow to a rapid rhythm. Your heart beats as if it might jump out of your chest at any moment. Butterflies are swarming in your stomach. Jittery legs have moved you from sitting on the bed to pacing the floor.

What is happening to me? Am I sick? Am I dying? Do I tell my parents? Are my friends going through this? Will someone use my anxiety against me? Will the teachers listen? Does God care?

Can you relate to these symptoms and questions? How can you be strong and courageous in the midst of feeling frozen during the real battle going on in your heart and mind?

Embrace God's presence by sitting and talking to Him through prayer. It is more powerful than the heavy feeling anxiety brings. When Moses spoke the above words from our scripture to the Israelites, he was reminding them that God would go before them and fight their battles. He doesn't leave them for a second. God is doing the same for you.

Keep moving. Work on one subject at a time and ask for help when confusion blocks your thinking. Take a deep breath to put your heart back in a slower pace. Run in place or take a walk to give the adrenaline a place to go. Drink some water to settle your stomach. Remind yourself God is near when Anxiety Elephants want to paralyze you in fear.

THE NEXT SMALL STEP

Write how anxiety makes you feel. In bold letters over your list, pen the words STRONG and COURAGEOUS as a reminder of who you are through God's presence.

PRAYER

Dear God, anxiety has scared me stiff. Help me have the courage to use one of these strategies and to remember You are always with me.

JOURNAL

....

....

....

....

....

....

....

....

....

....

EIGHT

"For you created my inmost being; you knit
me together in my mother's womb."

Psalm 139:13, NIV

Imagine you are walking out of the coffee house with the last few sips of your blended drink to-go. You check your phone notifications, and suddenly, you look up! A random stranger is texting while driving, unaware their car is speeding toward you. What do you do? Run? Kick at the car? Freeze while everything moves in slow motion? At this point, your amygdala has switched on to protect you and keep you alive. It houses your "fight or flight" response. Adrenaline rushes through your body to make your legs run as fast as possible.

God made every part of you amazing—including your brain. It performs different connections making you move, breathe, and think. In your brain, there are two important almond-shaped amygdalae (it's pronounced: a-mig-da-lay; singular is *amygdala).* The two amygdalae are at the base of your brain and are responsible for processing responses and memories associated with fear and other emotions.

Sometimes, the amygdala acts more like an overprotective parent. Do any of you have one of those? They know how important you are, so the thought of something being hazardous is treated like a real-life threatening situation. Anxiety comes into play, causing panic in your body over a thought, even if the fear behind that thought isn't based in reality.

When your brain goes into overdrive, God is not upset with you. When the fight, flight, or freeze response turns on when it isn't necessary, stop in your tracks and declare to your brain there is no imminent danger. You have permission to give direction to your body when the amygdala needs a jolt of reality. God knit you together with wisdom in your spirit to direct your flesh to walk at a calm pace.

THE NEXT SMALL STEP

When your brain switches into panic mode from inaccurately reading a situation, practice telling your amygdala you are safe.

PRAYER

Thank You, God, for knitting wisdom into me. Help me to use it when my flesh wants to go into a frenzy.

JOURNAL

....

....

....

....

....

....

....

....

....

....

NINE

"Cast all your anxiety on him because he cares for you."

1 Peter 5:7, NIV

Two catfish ponds awaited our arrival every year when we visited my grandparents in Mississippi. If you wanted to fish, you had to attempt to bait your own hook. My grandfather made sure he had a tub of squirmy worms ready to go while we cast our lines over and over to catch dinner. Grandma cooked everyone's prize while we debated who reeled in the big one. It was secretly a welcomed distraction from screens and the constant drama playing through my thoughts.

Fishermen during biblical times cast their nets much like we did on those fall days. Men would find their positions on the Sea of Galilee and prepare to throw the weighted mesh string overboard, hoping to find a school of fish trapped at the bottom. Their job was to catch as many fish as possible. All day they would throw out the net, pull it in, empty it, and hurl it out again.

Do you ever find anxiety annoying you with the constant overthinking about circumstances in your life or things you said that could be misinterpreted? Do you stare up at the popcorn ceiling, swimming in doubt over decisions you need to make? When anxious thoughts enter in, causing you to feel overwhelmed, worried, or afraid, take on the mindset of a fisherman.

First, you need a net or a fishing rod. This can be pen and paper, the note section on your phone, or sheet music to add a melody to your discomfort. When a thought enters your mind making you feel uneasy, write it down as fast as you can. Next, rip the paper into pieces. Find the garbage and cast it—throw it away. If you use your phone, once you have completed the note, delete it. For some, adding half notes and whole notes will give you an opportunity to change the tune in your head.

Repeat this process on a regular basis to retrieve the dreaded thoughts you no longer want to hear on repeat.

Getting rid of these beginning seeds of anxiety keeps it from taking over your mind and holding you hostage in fear. Peter reminds us that we can heave our angst-filled thoughts onto God as often as we need to because He cares. The battle going on in your head is important to Him. What do you need to share today?

THE NEXT SMALL STEP

Write one conversation you have over and over in
your mind that you want God to remove.

PRAYER

*Thank You, God, for helping me get rid of thoughts
trying to overpower me. I needed the reminder that I
can cast all my anxiety on You over and over.*

JOURNAL

....

....

....

....

....

....

TEN

"Do not be anxious about anything, but in
every situation, by prayer and petition, with
thanksgiving, present your requests to God."

Philippians 4:6, NIV

To be completely transparent, giving thanks is something I take for granted. I get caught up in what I don't have or what's not happening and forget the blessings all around me. Anxiety narrows my focus on the messiness of a situation. Instead of talking to God, I just complain. Seeing negative multiplies negative, but seeing His goodness exponentially shifts perspective.

Did you know that our brains cannot be anxious and thankful at the same time? This attitude of gratitude will trigger feel-good hormones in your body called serotonin and dopamine which block negative thoughts from being in charge.

By concentrating on positive things, you are rewiring your brain and teaching it what to focus on. The Lord knows the power of gratitude. He tells us to bring every situation to Him by prayer and thanksgiving.

How does this work?

When an anxious thought sneaks in, do a mental thankful check-in. Get as specific as possible. Tell God how thankful you are for the safe adults in your life, friends who help you with homework, your favorite caffeinated beverage, the used car you thought you might never get, etc. As you enter into prayer with thanksgiving, ask God to help you with whatever stressful situation you are facing. His peace will come and quiet your mind, bringing your heart back to a calm beat.

THE NEXT SMALL STEP

List three things you are thankful for. See how
many days you can continue this list.

PRAYER

*Thank You, God, for reminding me of the power of gratitude. It's
easy for me to see everything wrong. Help me to begin looking for
the good. I want to tell You I am thankful for (fill in the blank).*

JOURNAL

————

....

....

....

....

....

....

....

....

....

....

....

....

ELEVEN

"Finally, brothers and sisters, whatever is true, whatever
is noble, whatever is right, whatever is pure, whatever
is lovely, whatever is admirable—if anything is excellent
or praiseworthy—think about such things."

Philippians 4:8, NIV

Anxious thoughts are driven by the *What-If Zone.*

- What IF my friends laugh at my outfit?

- What IF my boyfriend/girlfriend breaks up with me?

- What IF I make the wrong decision about my future path?

- What IF I can't afford college or technical school?

- What IF I fail?

- What IF I don't get likes or views on my social media post?

- What IF I wake up with a zit before the homecoming dance?

- What IF . . . you fill in the blank.

Living in this place of constant dread about the future stops your ability to enjoy life at all. You find yourself stuck in mental thrillers playing out in your mind, where you, the main character, never have a happy ending. Focusing on things totally out of your control, that might not ever happen, is not God's blueprint for your thought life.

So, what can you do? How do you shift out of the mental weeds the Anxiety Elephants have tangled you in?

To exit the *What-If Zone,* it's time to practice alerting your thoughts to the *What-Is Zone.* When a "what-if" thought tries to enter your mind, stop. Before it can play out a scenario, test it with the list above: Is it true, pure, excellent, praiseworthy, lovely, or admirable?

If the answer is no, then search for a thought to replace it with, and keep yourself peacefully in the *What-Is Zone.*

Here, you discover things to focus on that are good, pure, and true. Staying in this region will keep your brain calm and it will thank you for doing your part in exiting unhealthy territory. Thinking on the areas listed in our verse gives you the master plan to stay grounded in your present moment and trust God with your future.

THE NEXT SMALL STEP

This is going to take intentional practice. Think about what you are thinking about, today. Use the list given to adjust your thoughts as needed. Don't give up if it doesn't work the first time.

PRAYER

God, I don't want to dwell on things I can't control.
Help me to focus on what IS and not what IF.

JOURNAL

....

....

....

....

....

....

....

....

TWELVE

"Commit to the Lord whatever you do,
and he will establish your plans."

Proverbs 16:3, NIV

Decisions, decisions, decisions. By the time *teen* is added to the end of your age, you are asked to make a lot of choices. I think we as adults forget all the choices you are obligated to make over the span of a few years. A variety of situations come your way varying from minor to major. You are thinking about what to put in your lunch to what high school track you will take in the second semester of eighth grade to which career path you want to travel before moving your tassel to the left.

Even deciding what time of the day to go to the bathroom to stay out of trouble can seem like a monumental task.

I thought I had to figure out the direction of my life alone. If I were to allow an adult into the pressure I was experiencing, I thought I would get into trouble for not knowing all the answers. The idea of failing God and completely messing up my life strangled me with fear. Pretending like it was no big deal and everything was under control emerged as a shaky strategy I slowly cracked beneath.

Do you find the burden of the decisions you need to produce to be heavy? Are you scared to pick the wrong option, so you choose no course of action? Are you worried to share the anxiousness you are experiencing with your parents or guardians, so you put on the "I totally got this" face?

Take a breath.

The good news is that you are not powerful enough to ruin all God has for you. The Lord is not asking you to make a go of life solo.

He wants to help you and relieve the weight of the world from your shoulders. The best course of action to take when a hefty decision comes your way, is to ask Him for help.

Ask God what He thinks is the best way for you to go. Surrender your thoughts on the situation to Him and wait. It is okay if you do not have an immediate answer. Get into the daily practice of committing big and small things to the Lord. As you allow Him to initiate next steps for your life, the boulder of decision-making falls into His hands. He will never give you the wrong answer.

THE NEXT SMALL STEP

Pick one decision you have been avoiding. Ask God what He would have you to do and write down thoughts that come through prayer. Talk to your parents about the gravity of this decision.

PRAYER

God, my boulder of decision is like a pebble in Your hands. I am committing my way and plans to You. Give me clarity to see Your answer.

JOURNAL

....

....

....

....

....

....

THIRTEEN

"See, I have chosen Bezalel son of Uri, the son of
Hur, of the tribe of Judah, and I have filled him with
the Spirit of God, with wisdom, with understanding,
with knowledge and with all kinds of skills."

Exodus 31:2-3, NIV

Bezalel had a pretty important job—building the Ark of the Covenant we read about in the Old Testament.

The Ark of the Covenant held the stone tablets with the Ten Commandments written on them by God, and the Mercy Seat was crafted to sit on top. Once a year, the high priest would enter the inner part of the tabernacle to sacrifice an animal as a payment for the sins committed by the people. When Jesus came, He became the ultimate one-and-done sacrifice for the forgiveness of our sins.

Bezalel was filled with all kinds of skills, but his skills were not like others's around him. Without these abilities, he would not have been part of this project. How horrible would it have been if Bezalel had neglected his skills because he was comparing himself to others?

There are times when Anxiety Elephants can cause us to compare ourselves to others and feel "less than." We analyze their social media posts seeing the filtered images and text they portray as a much better life next to our behind-the-scenes reality. The number of loyal followers and viral posts they share can cause us to diminish what God placed in us to offer to this world.

But we no longer have to allow someone else's highlight reel to define what we can offer this world.

Think about it like this. If puzzles only had outside pieces, we would never know what the entire picture looked like. Every piece is needed. If one is missing, it doesn't work. Those irregular, inner pieces are what add the beauty to the picture.

If your unique gifting did not walk on this earth, there would be an empty space no one else could fill. Just as God chose Bezalel, He chose you. Place this truth in your bio the next time the comparison game tries to steal your joy. Comparison is one competition you can quit and walk away from today.

THE NEXT SMALL STEP

Write down one thing you can do really well.

PRAYER

Thank you, God, for making me in a unique way. Help me to not allow social media to dictate thoughts about myself when You have already defined who I am.

JOURNAL

....

....

....

....

....

....

....

....

FOURTEEN

Jesus wept.

John 11:35, NIV

The newest text on your phone punches you in the gut, and you wet your toothpaste with your tears instead of the cold water from the faucet. Mom runs down the stairs to say good night, and you shut the door quickly before she can see your swollen eyes. You wait for the coast to clear to hide your face in your dark bedroom, ready to hug your secret misery. The next day, you stuff heartbreak into your backpack, embarrassed by the bawling session you had but refusing to let anyone know about your pain.

Jesus shows us it is okay to cry. He didn't run off when emotions got heavy. Jesus never belittled Himself or dismissed the sorrowful situation. There are no words in scripture where He apologizes for the way His remorse was shown.

Crying is not a sign of weakness. Being sad is not a sin. Feeling upset or having a bad day happens. You don't have to put pressure on yourself to appear happy and to have it all together all the time.

If you read all of the story in John 11, Jesus had lost His friend, Lazarus, and He was grieving. He also wept because of the great disbelief in the hearts of those around Mary and Martha, the sisters of Lazarus. They didn't believe Jesus could raise him from the dead. He proved them all wrong.

If Jesus can cry, you can too. Do you have something in your life you need to grieve? Have you lost a friend? Are you moving? Have your parents separated or divorced? Have the homework assignments piled up and you feel like you are collapsing under World War I and II? Is there a difficult situation going on at school? Are you getting ready to play a big rival and the pressure to perform well is coming from all directions? Is your family facing a financial challenge?

You no longer have to shut down your sadness. Let the tears flow and release the anxiety of keeping it all together.

THE NEXT SMALL STEP

Follow the example of Jesus. Time for an overdue cry.

PRAYER

Thank You, Jesus, for showing me it is okay to cry.

JOURNAL

....

....

....

....

....

....

....

....

....

....

FIFTEEN

"Carry each other's burdens, and in this
way you will fulfill the law of Christ."

Galatians 6:2, NIV

There is one word we all find difficulty using. One word plagues adults and teens alike. It is a life-changing word when we put it into action. Our enemy knows it shifts us out of the direction of isolating destruction. What is this powerful word?

HELP!

We convince ourselves we are supposed to figure it all out on our own. If we have problems or things are getting messed up, no one can know. People have enough to deal with in their own lives, so we shouldn't burden them with our troubling situations.

Lies . . . it's all lies, friends!

God wants other people walking beside us—walking beside you. The things you are facing at your age right now are beyond what my generation faced at this juncture of life. Technology has not only simplified things, but it has also added difficulty. Where we had the opportunity to walk away from a disheartening situation, your situations follow you around in the palm of your hand. Calling for *HELP* allows a troop of people to pull back the curtain of shame trying to suffocate you.

Helpers come in all forms. Counselors, doctors, teachers, parents, friends, pastors, and coaches are all people God has gently placed in your life to give you guidance and support. I know it's hard, but today is the day ... it's time to put those four letters into action.

THE NEXT SMALL STEP

Today, seek out a safe adult God has placed in your life to talk about hard things. Start with this statement: "I need your help."

PRAYER

Lord, today I choose to reach out for help. I know there is freedom in these four letters. Help me share this load with the safe adults You have established around me.

JOURNAL

....

....

....

....

....

....

....

....

....

....

....

....

SIXTEEN

"I waited patiently for the Lord; he turned to me and heard my cry. He lifted me out of the slimy pit, out of the mud and mire; he set my feet on a rock and gave me a firm place to stand."

Psalm 40:1-2, NIV

Do you remember a time in your life when you got stuck? I never got my head stuck anywhere, but my car was a different story. While my husband and I were dating, he followed me home one night from the movies. I do not remember why we drove separately, but I do remember it was a race to see who could arrive at my apartment first. Now, I don't want to brag, but I was winning. But as we went around the turn, things took a slight change.

I was going a tad too fast on a slick road. I spun into a small, grassy ditch inches away from a light post. My husband ran to make sure I was okay. By the grace of God, there was not a scratch on me or my car, but my back tire was stuck in the muddy grass. Panic set in, but we finally got me and my car out and safely home. No more racing.

Anxiety makes us feel the same way. When that elephant comes and plops down on your chest, a crushing feeling takes over and pushes you down. The harder you try to get out from under it, the more confused you become. You feel weighed down, almost like you are in a pit of quicksand.

How do you get out?

Treat the panic like real quicksand. Quicksand is a dense mixture of water and sand that forms into a solid-appearing, sinking substance. When you step into it, your feet slowly sink down. If you panic, it can cause you to go down faster. Researchers suggest the best way to get out of quicksand is to do the following: relax, take deep breaths, retreat slowly, rest, and repeat.

Try these steps the next time anxious feelings ambush you. By following this process, you will begin to feel God lifting you up and putting your feet on firm ground.

THE NEXT SMALL STEP

Find one thing you can do to help you relax
when you feel overwhelmed.

PRAYER

*Thank You, God, for simple steps to get out of
the anxiety quicksand when I feel stuck.*

JOURNAL

....

....

....

....

....

....

....

....

....

....

SEVENTEEN

"The righteous cry out, and the Lord hears them;
he delivers them from all their troubles."

Psalm 34:17, NIV

The constant pounding.

The constant berating.

The constant attacks.

The constant stomping.

It is a crushing feeling. The Anxiety Elephants come in undetected by anyone else around you. Punching you, pounding you, verbally attacking you. You might look like you are standing tall on the outside, but you are crushed into a million different pieces inside.

While all of this is happening, no one else knows what's going on inside you. No one hears the silent cries you barely let out. No one feels what you feel. No one sees the emotional bruises and pain you camouflage. Loneliness is the message Anxiety Elephants spew out to convince you that no one cares. Is there anyone out there who really understands what you are going through?

At my lowest point, this verse cracked the window open to my soul. I cried because it was as if God was reaching down and holding my face between His two gentle hands saying, "I'm here and I love you." He lifted my chin from the downward position it had been in for a long time. Close your eyes and imagine God is sitting in the room right now beside you doing the same for you.

God has more for you. He will show you this same gift of loving compassion as you ascend out from under Anxiety Elephants. He doesn't want you to be in that place any longer, experiencing pain alone.

Jesus came for the sick and hurting, which means you and me. He is near. Open up to Him today.

THE NEXT SMALL STEP

Close your eyes, sit, or kneel. Your Good Father wants to be the lifter of your head. He is cupping your face in His hands right now and saying, "I love you."

PRAYER

Father, I need Your love today. I am asking You to pull me close to You. Lift my head and wipe away my tears.

JOURNAL

....

....

....

....

....

....

....

....

....

....

EIGHTEEN

"Say to those with fearful hearts, 'Be strong, do not
fear; your God will come, he will come with vengeance;
with divine retribution he will come to save you.' "

Isaiah 35:4, NIV

When I was in the third grade, I cried so bad on a kiddie roller coaster that they stopped it so I could get off and stop ruining the experience for the other children. As a teenager, I fake-fainted because I didn't want to go through the haunted house with my friends and boyfriend. I was too scared to tell them I was afraid. The memory of the emergency worker carrying me out while I was clutching my ankle still plays through my mind. My dad worked for the railroad, so he would be gone for multiple days at a time. I would be fearful without him at home, especially during the night. Seeing a dentist chair in a movie or hearing the rotation of the drill still causes me to get anxious.

Fear filled my heart all the time when I was a teenager, and I didn't know what to do or how to respond. I never told anyone it was there. It is a lonely place being by yourself in constant alarm, always waiting for something terrible to happen.

Have you experienced fear like this? You might relate to some of the examples given, or maybe fear comes to you in different situations. Either way, it can still lead to a sad place.

Our verse reminds us to call on God and He will save us in those fearful moments. Prayer is our way of calling out to God. It is our lifeline we can use day or night. Talking to Jesus about fear is the right thing to do. It opens the door to let Him come in and help you.

THE NEXT SMALL STEP

What are your fears? Write them below. Read
Isaiah 35:4 and remind yourself that these fears
are powerless when God is your help.

PRAYER

*Jesus, I am coming to You with all my fears. Help me to stand
strong when fear tries to convince me I am powerless.*

JOURNAL

....

....

....

....

....

....

....

....

....

....

....

NINETEEN

"My dear brothers and sisters, take note of this:
Everyone should be quick to listen, slow to speak and
slow to become angry, because human anger does
not produce the righteousness that God desires."

James 1:19-20, NIV

Emotional outbursts follow in the dust of Anxiety Elephants. They explode onto the scene, and you can't explain what happened or where they came from. Random questions about lunch for the day or how the English test went are met with an eruption of tears. Your fist clenches and a deluge of inappropriate words follow after you miss the game-winning goal. Embarrassment surrounds you once the reality of these awkward situations set into motion.

Anxiety can bring out spontaneous reactions. When the emotional part of your brain is running the show, it will overreact if not kept in check. Trials can blast a plume of anger into situations when our minds are focused on the only outcome we deem appropriate. In the crucial moments leading up to the detonator going off, we are not listening or keeping our mouths shut. Instead, we are setting the scene for a massive blow-up leaving destruction in its path. Hurtful things are said or done you can't take back.

How do we avoid these flare-ups from being set off in our minds?

James gives us a two-step mental method to follow when an emotional timer is initiated.

First, be quick to listen. Our flesh tends to be sluggish in this directive. When we take a breath and tune in to seeking the way God would have us respond in frustrating circumstances, we are not looking to prove our point. Instead, we are waiting for additional information that will guide us to His solution.

Finally, being slow to speak and slow to anger turns off the remote to the emotional bomb ready to blow. Using the two ears God gave you will slow down your one mouth that may want to spout off. Peace will now respond in the place anxiety used to react.

THE NEXT SMALL STEP

Practice taking a breath when you feel angry emotions arise. Ask God to open your ears and close your mouth before you speak a harmful word.

PRAYER

God, I admit my anger gets the best of me at times. Forgive me for my outbursts, and help me to remember to be quick to listen and slow to speak.

JOURNAL

....

....

....

....

....

....

....

....

....

TWENTY

"Don't have anything to do with foolish and stupid arguments, because you know they produce quarrels."

2 Timothy 2:23, NIV

Do you ever find yourself scrolling the comment section of a feud going on between famous people on your favorite social media platform? The battle of words is typically birthed from a misunderstanding, gossip that has been spreading, or a statement taken out of context. The goal to get attention and be noticed comes with a price. Before you know it, a thread filled with controversy spills from filtered lives to real behind-the-scenes action.

During Timothy's time, false teachers spewed out their own fake truths. It would have been easy for him to get caught up in the drama instead of using his time and conversations to share the real truth of God's love. His opponents' goal was to pull him into a combat of words to distract people's hearts from hearing God's message of hope. In today's verse, Paul warned him not to allow these arguments to get him sidetracked from his calling.

When you see snaps of drama or read untrue mean tweets, how can you simply walk away from these stupid arguments?

Take a step back and ask yourself: is it worth your time to scroll and comment on someone's foolish statements that are simply trying to get a reaction out of you? If they don't get the desired outcome they want, they will move on.

Ultimately, Paul's warning prevents you from getting into unwanted drama that will linger through every area of your life. Remember, as believers, our responsibility is to show the kindness and love of Christ. Focusing on how He would respond to social media buzz will give you wisdom on when it is time to log out.

THE NEXT SMALL STEP

Instead of reading or watching drama play out on social media, unfollow those accounts that are spreading gossip. This will take time, but you will be grateful for an updated feed.

PRAYER

Dear Lord, help me to not get pulled into pointless arguments but to stay focused on spreading Your kindness and love.

JOURNAL

....

....

....

....

....

....

....

....

....

....

....

TWENTY-ONE

"I can do all this through him who gives me strength."

Philippians 4:13, NIV

There is one sport I really loved growing up ... basketball.

My brother and his friends would always include me in the game because I never really liked walking around the track talking during P.E. The ball would come my way quite a bit to shoot. Defense was never my favorite, but I would go hard when needed. They always treated me like an equal teammate in the game and let me contribute when I was on the court.

The time came to try out for the middle school team and eventually high school. I would love to tell you I tried out, broke records, and was the MVP, but my story ended during P.E. with my brother.

The anxiety I felt about playing in front of people, and the pressure of winning and losing, caused my heart to race out of my chest. I knew how our student section yelled at the visiting team and couldn't imagine being the one on the court under the brutal mockery. I was afraid people would make fun of me because of my cerebral palsy. Knowing what rejection and embarrassment felt like, I never tried out. Would I have been good? Well, we will never know.

Anxiety stole from me then and it is trying to steal from you now. God has strengthened you to do *all* things—including the very thing you are scared to do. What do you love to do, but the anxiety has paralyzed you? The only way to make fear disappear is to face it. Jesus is ready to give you the bravery to go forward. As you move ahead, your fear will begin to shrink—and Jesus' power within you becomes greater.

THE NEXT SMALL STEP

What is one activity you secretly love to do, but anxiety has tried to steal it from you? Ask a friend to help you face the unknown and give it a try. It just might be the outlet you need.

PRAYER

Thank You, Jesus, for giving me strength. Help me to live with no regrets and to have fun trying new things without focusing on the end result.

JOURNAL

....

....

....

....

....

....

....

....

....

....

....

....

TWENTY-TWO

"For he will command his angels concerning
you to guard you in all your ways."

Psalm 91:11, ESV

I was scared of the dark when I was a kid and even as a teenager .
. . who am I kidding, I am still scared of the dark as an adult! Dogs
barking late at night, trains blaring, and the house creaking. Up until
college, I slept with a clown night light that was holding balloons.
Believe it or not, he was a friendly face to see as I got under the
covers.

Bedtime anxiety still happens for many teenagers. It is not just
small children who experience Anxiety Elephants when it is time to
sleep. You go from being active and around people all day to dark
silence. Your parents close the door and say, "Sweet dreams," but
your thoughts are far from sweet. You hear the stomping feet in your
ears and see Anxiety Elephants pounding on your heart. You pull the
blanket up tight until you can't take it anymore.

Some yell out to their parents in fear. Others get up and grab a glass
of water with a late-night snack. Many will hide under the covers
until exhaustion sets in and their eyes finally close.

There is no judgment or shaming here for how Anxiety Elephants
attack you and cause you to react at night. I remember.

Changing your nightly room environment is a solution to put into
motion. Try sleeping with a small light on. There are several LED options safe to leave on while you sleep. Find glow-in-the-dark stars to
stick on your ceiling. Read a great book. Play worship music to keep
your mind on the Lord. Use a notebook to draw and allow creativity
to flow until your mind falls asleep. Open your Bible and write down
the scripture that speaks peace to your heart.

Hold onto this special verse when night comes and remember that God's angels are surrounding you.

THE NEXT SMALL STEP

Write one thing you would like to change during your nighttime routine. Start making these impactful changes now.

PRAYER

Thank You, God, for commanding Your angels to protect me.

JOURNAL

....

....

....

....

....

....

....

....

....

....

....

TWENTY-THREE

"When you lie down, you will not be afraid; when
you lie down, your sleep will be sweet."

Proverbs 3:24, NIV

Sleep! Where are you?!? I look for you night after night, and you are nowhere to be found. Why have you left me?

Raise your hand if you struggle with going to sleep? It is frustrating, especially when you have a big test or project you need to be prepared for, but your mind is exhausted. You want to close your eyes and drift off to Sleepy Town, but the harder you try, the farther away it retreats. You find yourself avoiding bedtime because your mind races with thoughts of tasks you didn't complete. Then, your heart beats to the pounding of a herd of elephants moving through the African savanna.

Sweet sleep sounds nice, but how do you get there?

Instead of listening to true crime podcasts before bedtime, search for voices a little more lighthearted. Watching scary things on TV can leave vivid pictures in your mind. Find shows filled with joy and hilarious story lines. Laughter really is medicine for your soul. Spend time in worship and prayer, allowing God's powerful love to melt the anxieties in your heart.

Write down your anxious thoughts so that they will stop bombarding your mind. Release them to God in prayer. Drinking sleepy-time tea and taking an Epsom salt bath will help close your tired eyes.

Rest in the truth that God handles all of your cares and concerns and nothing you face will happen out of His sight. Write down the above scripture and others to focus your mind and heart on God and not on all the events of the day. God's word is a very powerful source for every area of your life, including sleep.

It's time for sleep to come back home to you.

THE NEXT SMALL STEP

Do a quick internet search for scriptures on sleep. Write them down and pick one to memorize before you drift off into sweet sleep. Put it above your bed to see before closing your eyes.

PRAYER

God, I am really tired. I need help getting rest.
I am asking You for sweet sleep.

JOURNAL

....

....

....

....

....

....

....

....

....

....

TWENTY-FOUR

"We demolish arguments and every pretension that sets
itself up against the knowledge of God, and we take
captive every thought to make it obedient to Christ."

2 Corinthians 10:5, NIV

Anxiety Elephants can take your thoughts to some frightening places. Once one scary thought gets cemented in your head, an alarming notion takes over and triggers an entire sequence of unfortunate events. Before you know it, you are in complete panic mode, unable to breath, unable to move, unable to speak. All this stems from one single thought.

Our minds are powerful. What we think about affects every part of our lives, which is how anxiety can have such a strong hold. No one can see what's happening in our heads, so it's easier to conceal. But the more we cover up anxious thoughts, the bigger they become.

How can you change your daily thoughts?

STOP. Stop by action or say *stop* in your head. Don't allow the thought coming into your mind to take root. You get to be in charge of your brain. Accept ownership of what is trying to enter and intentionally throw up a red sign to keep it from going any further.

After you **STOP** anxious thoughts from taking root, take them **CAPTIVE.** One way to capture anxious thoughts is to write all of your feelings down. Document what is bombarding your mind. Write until you can no longer hear your fears.

Finally, **REPLACE** old thoughts with new ones. If we don't put something else in our minds, we are left with empty space. We don't want our anxious thoughts to return and bring friends. Say life-giving thoughts out loud so your mind hears the shift you have made in your heart.

Overcoming anxiety is not an overnight fix. But once you get the hang of taking thoughts captive, it will happen so quickly the Anxiety Elephants won't know what hit them.

THE NEXT SMALL STEP

Practice the **Stop, Captive, Replace** method below.
Identify a repetitive anxious thought, take it captive
by writing it below, and replace it with truth.

PRAYER

Lord, help me to take bad thoughts captive and
replace them with life-giving truth!

JOURNAL

....

....

....

....

....

....

....

....

TWENTY-FIVE

"But the Lord God called to the man, 'Where are
you?' He answered, 'I heard you in the garden, and
I was afraid because I was naked; so I hid.' "

Genesis 3:9-10, NIV

Did you know we have been hiding since the beginning of time? Early on, Adam and Eve hid in the Garden of Eden. When the devil—in the form of a serpent—planted a seed of doubt in Eve's head, she began to ponder if God truly told them not to eat fruit from the tree in the middle of the garden. Even though God told them they would die, the crafty serpent convinced her this was not the case. He told her she would actually become like God if she ate from that tree.

When Eve began to see the fruit the way Satan portrayed it, she took a bite. Adam stood next to her, enjoying the same fruit. This changed things forever. As our verses tell us, their eyes were opened after this grave decision to disobey God. He came into the garden looking for them, and Adam said, "I was afraid, so I hid." Fear caused them to hide.

Even though they were hiding, God searched for them. He called out to Adam and Eve. He is calling out to you.

Facing the fear you have of Anxiety Elephants attacking you may be one of the hardest things you have ever done. I remember the first time I told people I was dealing with anxiety. My biggest fear was that they would reject me and turn their backs on me.

The opposite happened.

As I waited for the mean words to come, something else happened. They hugged me. They let me talk and tell what was really going on in my heart, body, and soul. Some knew exactly what I was describing, and others sat quietly without judging.

When you are ready to share it all, there will be people ready to listen. More importantly, God will be there waiting with open arms.

THE NEXT SMALL STEP

No more hiding. Talk about your anxiety. Remember,
God is looking for you because He loves you.

PRAYER

*I will not hide any longer, God. It's time to come
clean and talk to You and my parents.*

JOURNAL

....

....

....

....

....

....

....

....

....

TWENTY-SIX

"What good is it for someone to gain the
whole world, yet forfeit their soul?"

Mark 8:36, NIV

LOSER.

You walk into the bathroom to check your hair and see a new name added to the stall graffiti. It's yours. This descriptive word cuts a little deeper knowing the circumstances around it. Your friends have turned their backs on you. No more prom-posal expected from your boyfriend ... er, ex-boyfriend. All you had to do was continue to break curfew, go to the parties with the alcohol, and sneak money out of your mom's purse to pay for your share of supplies. Suddenly, none of those things satisfy you anymore. You lie in your bed at night with confused thoughts, wondering if you have to continue to do all these things to be viewed acceptable. All the other high schoolers are pretending to be something they aren't, but you just can't keep up the facade anymore. You have already labeled yourself a loser, but to see it etched in a swinging door makes it feel as if this new definition of yourself is true.

God knows every wrong you have done or will do. He knew you would not be perfect. God doesn't hold struggles against you. In fact, He knew the troubles you were going to face on this earth, including anxiety. Knowing the hard things ahead, He wanted to make sure you did not have to do life alone.

God wants you to know, above all else, that *YOU* are loved by Him. He doesn't view you as a loser. Jesus was willing to lose His own life so you would find eternal life for your soul.

Our Heavenly Father did the only thing He could do to make a way for you to have a relationship and eternal life with Him—He gave up His one and only Son. Jesus came to die on the cross for our sins. Our Savior did this out of obedience to the Father and love for you and me.

You can continue turning the pages of each new day knowing there is nothing that can separate you from God, not even an Anxiety Elephant.

If you have never asked Jesus into your heart, today can be the day of your salvation. Confess with your mouth and believe with your heart that Jesus is Lord and you shall be saved (Romans 10:9).

THE NEXT SMALL STEP

This will be the most important next step you will ever take. If you haven't made Christ the Savior of your life and surrendered your soul, you can at this moment.

PRAYER

Dear Jesus, I believe You died on the cross for my sins. I ask You to forgive me of my sins and cleanse my heart. Come into my heart and life. I believe You are my Savior and Lord.

JOURNAL

....

....

....

....

....

....

TWENTY-SEVEN

"Can any one of you by worrying add
a single hour to your life?"

Matthew 6:27, NIV

Up at the plate waiting for the perfect pitch . . . but what if you miss? Strike one, strike two, strike three, YOU'RE OUT.

You wait for that one list or roster to open up where you can know, without a doubt, you will make it and be the best . . . you are still waiting.

You sit and study the vocabulary over and over, worried of what might happen if you make less than an A.

You don't turn in the homework assignment and pretend you don't care. But the truth is, you are embarrassed because you really didn't understand what to do and you are worried about the response.

Perfection is not required to walk the journey God has for you. The worry of getting it right every single time is stealing life away from you. The good news is that God knew you wouldn't get it right every time. He never put the requirement of perfection on us, so you can take it off of yourself. All you need is a willingness to obey and the faith to take steps forward, baby and giant, with lots of grace as your companion.

A practical tool many counselors use is called "The Worry Box." You can create this by using a shoebox. Decorate it with anything you want from dried noodles to gobs of glitter. Cut a hole in the middle big enough for slips of paper to fit through. When worry thoughts come attacking, physically get rid of them. Write them down and throw them into The Worry Box. This visual gives you a tool to use to let go of worry so you can enjoy life the way God desires for you.

THE NEXT SMALL STEP

Create your own Worry Box.

PRAYER

I am giving my worries to You, Lord.

JOURNAL

....

....

....

....

....

....

....

....

....

....

....

TWENTY-EIGHT

"For the Spirit God gave us does not make us timid,
but gives us power, love and self-discipline."

2 Timothy 1:7, NIV

Fear has been one of the biggest triggers to call Anxiety Elephants after me.

Traces of this enemy have wiggled into different moments of my life. Sleeping in the dark was a no-go for me in middle school, so I slept with a light on to stop darkness from surrounding me. Riding on roller coasters was never on my "fun list"—that is, until I met my husband. I cried on the first one we rode together—don't tell him!

Triggers signal Anxiety Elephants to show up and pick on your body, mind, and soul. But unless you are aware of what these signals are, you don't realize they have been activated until the Elephants are already beating you up.

What could trigger your anxiety? Here are some examples of common Anxiety Elephant signals:

- Stress level increases because of tests or peer pressure
- Lack of sleep
- Socializing or lack of socializing (isolation)
- Types of food, drink, or other outside influences on your body and mind
- A busy after-school schedule
- Social media

Recognizing your triggers now puts the power back in your hands. By knowing ahead of time what things may set you off, you can stop the sneak attack of Anxiety Elephants. Remind yourself in those moments what type of mind and spirit God has given you. Timothy makes it clear we no longer have a spirit of cowardice looming inside.

THE NEXT SMALL STEP

List your triggers like we did in the list above. How can you use this information to have a sound mind?

PRAYER

Thank You, God, for reminding me that I do not have a spirit of fear, and that these triggers do not control me. Help me to walk in power, love, and with a sound mind.

JOURNAL

....

....

....

....

....

....

....

....

....

TWENTY-NINE

"And we know that in all things God works for
the good of those who love him, who have
been called according to his purpose."

Romans 8:28, NIV

God wastes nothing in your life. He will use it all for good, including this battle with anxiety. He takes what the enemy meant to use as a negative and turns it into a positive. Through the assault of all the emotions and feelings trying to control your life, you are learning how to turn towards the Lord and seek direction from Him.

Our verse reminds me of the account of Jesus feeding the five thousand in the four Gospels. He is surrounded by lots of people who are becoming hangry. Never a good combination. He tells the disciples to go search for food to feed the families who have been sitting and listening all day. The only sustenance they discover is a small lunch containing five loaves of bread and two fish, held by a little boy. Somehow, this was supposed to feed the massive crowd. This young child gave all he had, and Jesus performed a miracle. Good came out of this meal meant for one.

As you place the anxiety, which is trying to steal your life, into God's hands, He will begin to do a mighty work. The tools He has placed in your mind and heart will become natural weapons for you to use against the heavy weight of the Elephant trying a sneak attack.

Not only has He given you power over this enemy, but He will give you opportunities to help others. You have friends facing the same emotions, feelings, and triggers you have. They are afraid. God will equip you and prepare you to teach them what you are learning.

THE NEXT SMALL STEP

Who could benefit from what you have learned so far? Brainstorm and pray for opportunities to share these strategies with them.

PRAYER

God, thank You for giving me tools and guidance on how to overcome anxiety. Who is a friend in need of the same thing?

JOURNAL

....

....

....

....

....

....

....

....

....

....

....

THIRTY

"So do not fear, for I am with you; do not be dismayed,
for I am your God. I will strengthen you and help you;
I will uphold you with my righteous right hand."

Isaiah 41:10, NIV

Fear took fun moments out of my life. Finding a creative excuse to avoid sleepover parties was not easy, but I managed. Going to bed at night made me feel jittery and uneasy. I checked under my bed for monsters and carefully examined the shadows on the wall. I missed out on youth trips early on because I was nervous about going places I had never been. An alarm would go off in my head causing me to say NO to any new experience without even considering the value it might add to my life.

The Anxiety Elephants never grow tired of putting scary thoughts in your brain. Fear takes what you see and manipulates it into something completely untrue.

Where have Anxiety Elephants taken your mind in fear? How do you stand your ground when fear comes?

First, begin to speak God's word out loud and remind fear who your God is. Our scripture today is a great weapon to use. Memorize it and hide it in your heart.

Next, when fear says you can't do something, face your fear and go for it. Maybe you are wanting to go out for an after-school team or audition for the school play. Whatever it is, you got this!

Finally, make friendships with other teens you can reach out to and share your fearful thoughts with. You might be surprised and relieved to hear them say they are feeling the same thing.

We do not have a reason to fear since we are on the eternal winning team. The threats of this world will never be able to destroy us or our security in Christ. Trusting in Him and trusting that He is in control and takes care of us helps us to overcome fear.

THE NEXT SMALL STEP

Write today's scripture down and place it on your bathroom mirror. Pick something small you have been afraid to do and go tackle it.

PRAYER

Thank You, God, that I have nothing to fear with You on my side. Thank You for strengthening me to crush these Anxiety Elephants and their scare tactics. They no longer have power over me.

JOURNAL

....

....

....

....

....

....

....

....

....

THIRTY-ONE

"You intended to harm me, but God intended it for good to accomplish what is now being done, the saving of many lives."

Genesis 50:20, NIV

His own brothers threw him into a pit. Can you imagine? Joseph was sold as a slave by his siblings. He had no control over the events that were about to take place, but he knew he could trust in God. He ended up serving a man named Potiphar, got thrown into jail, and finally ended up in front of Pharaoh to interpret two dreams. Joseph spoke of the harvest coming and warned of the famine to follow. God used him to make sure a plan was in place to have food for everyone. He was put in charge of the whole land of Egypt as Pharaoh's second-in-command. Thirteen years later, his brothers would come to Egypt for food and Joseph was given the opportunity to serve them and reunite with his father. Our scripture today is the words Joseph spoke to his brothers when they became afraid of his newfound power.

What do you do when something upsetting comes, and you can't control the outcome?

Ultimately, God is in control of everything, and we can trust Him. This is good news for us. We don't have to allow worry to consume us and make us feel like we are spiraling out of control. One thing that will help when this out-of-control feeling comes is to focus on what you can control.

We can control our attitude, our thoughts, and the words we say. Instead of thinking of the worst-case scenario, think of a positive one. Use your words to speak about a potentially encouraging outcome. Choose to allow your attitude to be focused on the good and not always looking for the bad. Leave the rest up to God.

By releasing yourself from the role of Savior-in-Chief, relief will fill your heart and mind. You were never meant to control everything.

THE NEXT SMALL STEP

Find a stress ball as a reminder to release control.
You could even get in touch with your childhood
and use play dough as a stress reliever.

PRAYER

*Thank You, God, for being in control. It is a relief
to know I don't have to do Your job.*

JOURNAL

....

....

....

....

....

....

....

....

....

....

THIRTY-TWO

"Do not be misled: 'Bad company corrupts good character.'"

1 Corinthians 15:33, NIV

Have your parents ever told you that you will become like those you hang around? I know, when they tell you those eye-roll inducing statements, you don't like them. We didn't like it when our parents told us those one-liners either, so I do get it. But it is only shared from a place of experience in hopes you will learn from our mistakes.

Finding your friend group amongst the lockers in middle school and high school is not the easiest hallway to navigate. Anxiety can be at an all-time high as every possible doomsday scenario plays out across your mind. You pass by other teenagers with the same goofy stare on their face—their imagination is playing out the exact same things. You are gripped by the fear of rejection and the what-ifs of not being part of the "cool kids" or popular group.

What is the most difficult thing for you as you are navigating these social pathways?

Our verse today does not sugarcoat what you need to know. Your friend group does matter. There is power in numbers. If the majority of your close friends are choosing to live life in a way that is not honoring to what God's word teaches, their behavior will have an open door to corrupt your belief system. If your group of friends is following the same guidelines you are striving to live by, then they can be a valuable accountability system to you and you to them.

I'm not saying to only hang out with Christians and shun everyone else. What I do want you to see is that your close friendships are important.

If we were to get honest, how would you rate the morals of your friend group? Is the company you keep helping you to seek God or to run from Him? If you were to look at how you participate in friendships, would you say you are helping your friends seek the Lord or pulling them away?

This is not a day of condemnation but instead one of evaluation. As the years go by, you will be looking at who you connect to and if healthy boundaries need to be put into place. God wants all of us to step back and ask ourselves these questions.

THE NEXT SMALL STEP

How is your friend group? What is one change you
need to make within yourself or the group?

PRAYER

*Dear Lord, help me to have an honest look at those I'm closest
to. Reveal to me if I am pulling my friends away from You
instead of helping them draw near to Your presence.*

JOURNAL

....

....

....

....

....

....

....

THIRTY-THREE

"Do not be afraid of them; the Lord your
God himself will fight for you."

Deuteronomy 3:22, NIV

Everywhere I turned, he was there. He always made sure to find a seat close to me at church, and if he saw me in the fifth-grade hallway, there was no getting away. This boy would make fun of how I talked, how I answered questions; he would pick on anything he could find.

One day, I woke up with terrible migraines. Anyone else out there experience those? I had been dealing with headaches, but nothing like this. All of a sudden, I realized my vision was blurry on the sides. Straight ahead was crystal clear, but I was seeing little silver stars through my peripheral vision.

While at the doctor, he asked me one simple question: "Is someone bullying you at school?" His question ripped the tape off of the secret I had been holding in. The words came out faster than I could think. My parents learned about the bullying at that moment along with the doctor. As I shared, relief came, and my eyesight went back to normal.

I was so anxious about seeing this bully and what he would do, that it caused harm to my body. I walked around tense and on eggshells six days a week. Instead of telling someone, I felt that pushing it down inside was easier. But eventually my body set off an alarm from holding on to all of this negativity.

This may be a hard question to answer, but is someone bullying you at school? Is it causing you to feel stomach pain, headaches, a rapid heartbeat, or constant nervousness?

If you are being bullied, the right thing to do is to tell someone. It is not wrong or snitching. There are adults who want to help you. For the health of your body and mind, they need to know.

The Lord is also fighting on your behalf. With Him at your side, you can stand up to the bully. Your voice may crack, and your words might shake, but when they see your boldness, it will make a difference.

THE NEXT SMALL STEP

Share with your parents or a trusted adult about bullying.

PRAYER

Dear God, give me courage to tell someone about being bullied. This is not a healthy way for me to live, and I want to stop being afraid.

JOURNAL

....

....

....

....

....

....

....

....

THIRTY-FOUR

"Be alert and of sober mind. Your enemy the devil prowls around like a roaring lion looking for someone to devour."

1 Peter 5:8, NIV

You and I have a real enemy.

The devil attacks because he wants you to be silent. He uses the weapon of shame. When you're quiet about this inner struggle, it's easier for him to whisper humiliation over your heart. He doesn't want you to talk about the anxiety you experience and how it makes you feel. Our enemy wants you to think you are the only one, so there's no reason to share.

This tool of shame makes you feel embarrassed and small. It causes weird sensations in the pit of your stomach from the mean thoughts you have about yourself. Satan runs these untrue statements through your mind and keeps you hidden behind an invisible wall of doubt so he can attack without anyone seeing.

He is a liar.

You are not the only one he uses this tactic on. What you are experiencing is real. This is not made up in your head. It is a big deal, and we are not going to dismiss it and pretend that ignoring it makes it go away.

How can you be alert and of sober mind? Stop pressing your thoughts and emotions down. It's clogging your logic and allowing your emotions to take control and misinterpret real-life situations. Acknowledge what is in front of you and what is happening inside.

Let the walls down and share your struggles with people who can help and hold you accountable. Accountability is not meant to shame you. Accountability is there to grow you and stretch you into all God has created you to be. When you are no longer isolated, your enemy will have a harder time attacking. There is power in numbers.

THE NEXT SMALL STEP

Write the name of one person below you can talk
with about being your accountability partner.

PRAYER

*Thank You, God, for the people who love me. Help me to
share my emotions and no longer push them down. I realize
having accountability protects me from the enemy.*

JOURNAL

....

....

....

....

....

....

....

....

....

....

THIRTY-FIVE

"For we are God's handiwork, created in Christ Jesus to do good works, which God prepared in advance for us to do."

Ephesians 2:10, NIV

When you wake up in the morning, what are the first thoughts you say to yourself? Are you telling yourself what you are not and who you will never be? Have you forgotten how much time God spent making you and breathing life into you?

Think about this—the skillful work of our Master Craftsman created every fiber of our beings. We matter so much to him, He made sure we were not a duplicate of any other person. Not only did He think about every part of you as He shaped and knitted you together, but He was also thinking about His plan being set into motion before you let out your first cry. The Lord thought about YOUR PURPOSE as He was creating you ON PURPOSE.

To Him, you were worth the work and time He put into every cell of your DNA because you matter and the works He has prepared for you are important.

The time has come for you to speak life over yourself. Your body and mind are listening. They interpret your words through actions and reactions. Negative talk breeds negative action. To see a change in your day-to-day self, change your internal dialogue. Be conscientious and intentional with the words you speak to yourself.

Going from a defeatist mindset to an overcomer mindset is going to take practice. There may be moments where the belief is not there and you have to ask God to help your unbelief. I still do this too. You will not get this right the first time, but repetition will be your friend. And there's no time like the present to start.

THE NEXT SMALL STEP

Take a fun selfie. Name characteristics you like about
yourself. It could be your smile, a talent you have,
the way you make people laugh—anything.

PRAYER

*God, I haven't really taken the time to think on how You took
Your time creating me on purpose for a purpose. Help me to
speak words of life over myself today and believe them.*

JOURNAL

....

....

....

....

....

....

....

....

....

....

....

THIRTY-SIX

"For God did not send his Son into the world to condemn the world, but to save the world through him."

John 3:17, NIV

We all have one bully in our life who follows us everywhere we go. It constantly puts us down when we sleep and when we get ready for a new day. This bully speaks hateful words. It tells us all the things we should be doing because others are doing them. This belittling voice speaks louder than any cheerleader with a megaphone. It says bully statements like . . .

You should be as good a student as she is.

You should be able to do it by yourself.

You shouldn't battle anxiety.

You should be the star of the football team and not sitting on the bench.

You shouldn't fail.

You should make an A on every test.

Are you ready to hear who this bully is who keeps attacking you?

It's **you.** Your biggest bully is yourself. We are our own worst critics.

Freedom from shame and condemnation come as we read today's scripture. It was never God's plan to send Jesus here wagging a finger of disappointment in our faces. His mission was one of rescue. He was sent to save us.

How can you stop "should-ing" on yourself?

Allow the love and forgiveness found in Christ to penetrate your heart. Evict any poisonous thoughts invading your mind. Combat lies with the truth of who you are from God's word:

- *A friend of Jesus.* (John 15:15)
- *Accepted by Christ.* (Romans 15:7)
- *Chosen, holy, and blameless before God.* (Ephesians 1:4)
- *God's workmanship created to produce good works.* (Ephesians 2:10)

Finally, believe. Believe these things are not just true about others, but that they are true for you.

It's time to silence your bully.

THE NEXT SMALL STEP

Every time the "should" bully attacks, fight it with TRUTH. Remind the bully exactly who you are. Don't back down. Pick one of the scriptures shared to help you dig your heels in and fight!

PRAYER

Thank You, Jesus, for giving me TRUTH. Help me to not listen to the "should" bully anymore.

JOURNAL

....

....

....

....

....

....

THIRTY-SEVEN

"He said to her, 'Daughter, your faith has healed you.
Go in peace and be freed from your suffering.' "

Mark 5:34, NIV

Imagine you are hanging out with friends. You have an intense game of volleyball going on outside when you get spiked in the face. The blood gushes from your nostrils after your nose blocked the game-winning point. Your mom runs to get a rag and tells you to hold your head back . . . for twelve years. How uncomfortable would that be? How much life would you miss out on because of this bloody situation?

The woman in our verse went through this very thing. She had a blood disease causing her to miss out on life for twelve years. She was isolated away from her family and friends. She couldn't come out and be a part of celebrations or normal day-to-day activities. No one could relate to what she was going through or understand her fear and emotions. Doctors could not help her, and she had lost all of her money seeking out their potions and remedies. Family and friends had turned their backs on her. Her culture defined her as unclean and unwanted.

Then, she heard about a man named Jesus coming to her town. She heard about His miracles. She risked it all, down to her life, for a moment to reach out and touch Him. She knew if she was caught, she could be killed. Stepping out of her mental and physical prison, she chose to believe Jesus could set her free.

Jesus was very clear when He said that HER FAITH made her well. A small act of faith, even in her weakness, is what healed her. Hebrews 11:1 describes faith as having confidence in what we hope for and assurance about what we do not see. She walked towards Jesus believing He would heal her without any physical proof. He not only healed her physical pain but her mental anguish as well. Her risk led to total recovery.

Your faith is powerful like the wind. You can't see it, but you can feel it. Use faith to reach out to Jesus and believe for Him to do something amazing in your life. Faith can move mountains. Even the mountains looking like elephants.

THE NEXT SMALL STEP

Reach out in FAITH today and ask God to heal you and to help you overcome this mountain of anxiety.

PRAYER

God, I am taking a risk and asking You to do what only You can do in my heart and mind. I am reaching out in faith, asking You for complete healing.

JOURNAL

....

....

....

....

....

....

....

....

THIRTY-EIGHT

"Trust in the Lord with all your heart and lean not
on your own understanding; in all your ways submit
to him, and he will make your paths straight."

Proverbs 3:5-6, NIV

Confession time! I am a MAJOR control freak!

This is slightly embarrassing, but I feel like we have been through a lot together over these pages, so why hold back now? Here it goes . . . I will look up the ending to a movie so I can control my response! I will never forget going to a movie on opening night with my husband. We had watched all the other movies in the series, and we could not wait to see how these superheroes were going to bring back their friends and defeat the ultimate bad guy. By the end, everyone was crying while I enjoyed my candy. (Don't worry. I don't share the ending with others and ruin it for them.)

At this point you guys are either laughing at me, laughing with me, or laughing at yourself because you do the same thing! I really hope it is the last one for at least one of you, so I am not the only one.

We feel that our way and understanding is always right. If it doesn't go the way we think it should or if a kink is thrown into the plan, what do we do? We freak out! We panic and freely open the gate to let Anxiety Elephants come in and add fuel to the fire we started.

Some of the anxiety we experience, at times, is because we have put ourselves in specific situations.

You can take pressure off of yourself today! Not everything is supposed to be within your control. God has a better view of things for your life. You can trust in what He sees. Acknowledge Him and seek

Him first. You do not have to figure out the next five giant steps before you take the next baby step anymore.

THE NEXT SMALL STEP

Ask God for advice. Ask Him how He wants you to fight back when Anxiety Elephants come at you. Give Him back the controls and begin focusing on the next small step He gives you.

PRAYER

Guide my steps, Lord. When I get frozen in anxiousness over the next few steps ahead, remind me that all You are asking me to do is to take one step at a time.

JOURNAL

....

....

....

....

....

....

....

....

....

THIRTY-NINE

"God is our refuge and strength, an ever-present help in trouble."

Psalm 46:1, NIV

The world of social media and conversations through the computer screen came to life when I was a teenager. We would all gather around our computers on Friday nights waiting to hear the dial-up connection from our phone lines finally connect with a loud ding to the early days of Internet. Yes, you read that correctly—phones used to be connected to the wall with a cord from the kitchen to your room, and checking our email was an ordeal.

No one knew the threats sneaking through those screens. Cyberbullying has become a real problem attacking your generation. Words and pictures are sent from phones and computers that no one would ever say to a person's face. Keyboard warriors can hide behind anonymous apps while they make life miserable for others.

Some of you may have experienced or are experiencing getting picked on through social media, group texts, and other platforms designed to hold the message for a few short hours before it disappears.

A message may leave the app, but it doesn't leave your heart. The words become etched into your brain, causing a pain difficult to explain. Online bullying affects boys and girls. Daily, hurtful messages go out across the world, harming those your age. The truth is, they may exit your devices after twenty-four hours, but they never escape the internet. If a future employer, police officer, or college admissions office wants to find posts, they will be able to find things you may have forgotten but the world wide web will hold forever.

God is a refuge, a safe place for you to turn to in times of trouble—even when you're being cyberbullied. You can talk to Him about the hurtful things happening. He also wants you to talk to the adults placed in your life to help. You are not being a blabbermouth by sharing demeaning statements being said through private messages.

Maybe you are reading this, and you feel some conviction because you aren't the one being bullied but the one choosing to bully others. You didn't realize the harm it was causing until now. As the Holy Spirit is gently showing you the wrong actions you have taken, use this moment to do the right thing and confess.

THE NEXT SMALL STEP

You don't have to be silent anymore. Talk to a trusted
adult about being bullied. If you are convicted about
how you have treated someone, apologize.

PRAYER

*I'm struggling with a bully. Give me courage, Lord,
to speak up and allow adults to help.*

JOURNAL

....

....

....

....

....

....

....

FORTY

"Therefore do not worry about tomorrow, for tomorrow will worry about itself. Each day has enough trouble of its own."

Matthew 6:34, NIV

Oftentimes, worry and anxiety come together. Have you noticed this for yourself? Worry is a symptom many experience when Anxiety Elephants attack with constant thoughts about what might happen in possible scenarios. I wanted to see how the dictionary's definition of worry lined up with what the Bible says. Merriam-Webster's dictionary says worry is mental distress resulting from concern usually anticipated; anxiety.[2]

Through a website called BibleGateway.com, I discovered a dictionary of Bible themes[3] and found worry. They describe worry as a sense of uneasiness and anxiety about the future. Both definitions reveal to us how our thoughts can go into worry mode when we are thinking too far in the future, trying to figure out outcomes of a scenario that probably won't happen, instead of trusting God with what each day brings.

What do you find yourself worrying about today that is about the future? It can be easy for some of us to work up a mental frenzy over something that hasn't happened. The worst-case scenario has already played out in our minds, and the end credits are running while our hearts are racing.

Jesus reminds us to keep our thoughts centered on right now. What you have going on today needs your attention instead of what could be weeks or months from now.

When you find your mind going into the future, ground your feet back into reality by using the senses God gave you: sight, taste, hearing, smell, and touch.

What is one thing you can see in front of you?

What is something you can taste?

What is one noise you can hear?

What is one thing you can smell?

What is one item you can touch?

By doing this, you are brought back to what is really going on around you. God equipped us with these natural skills to stay out of outlandish pictures wanting to steal the here and now.

THE NEXT SMALL STEP

Practice putting your senses to work. What can you
see, hear, taste, smell, and touch right now?

PRAYER

*Thank You, God, for giving me built-in senses
to bring me back to reality.*

JOURNAL

....

....

....

....

....

....

....

FORTY-ONE

"But those who hope in the Lord will renew their strength. They will soar on wings like eagles; they will run and not grow weary, they will walk and not be faint."

Isaiah 40:31, NIV

The bell rings, and it is time for lunch. Pandemonium traps you as the doors open to every classroom and the hallway is filled with noise and movements out of your control. You are squeezing your lunch bag a little tighter as you slowly move to an exit. You're laughing at the random joke you heard passing by classmates to hide your heart beating out of your chest. By the time you make it to your cafeteria seat, you are mentally collapsing while still trying to problem-solve how to make it through the last few periods of the day.

After an anxiety attack, exhaustion sets in. You are tired and embarrassed. The hardest part is that no one is aware of everything happening inside you, so they can't understand why you feel so weak. All they see is someone with a smile on their face moving through life like them.

Hope is a steadfast presence in these chaotic moments. It paves the path to believing change can happen. Hope fuels an inner strength inside us that we almost forgot God placed there. This means power is accessible even if it's not instantly felt.

By turning to hope, we find our strength renewed to get up and go again. Just as an eagle can hold his wings out and ride on the wind with no effort, hope lifts us up—little effort is required on our part as God carries us through.

Even if you still feel a little weary, He won't allow you to faint. When you lean on hope in the Lord, you don't need much to make it through the day. A small mustard seed of faith will do.

THE NEXT SMALL STEP

When everything feels out of control around you, instead of moving into panic, focus your thoughts on what you can control.

PRAYER

God, help me to cling to hope when exhaustion sets in.
Just as an eagle soars on the wind and waits for renewal,
I will do the same as I wait on Your strength to restore
me to make it through the next part of my day.

JOURNAL

....

....

....

....

....

....

....

....

....

....

....

....

FORTY-TWO

"Rejoice always, pray continually, give thanks in all circumstances; for this is God's will for you in Christ Jesus."

1 Thessalonians 5:16-18, NIV

I love when scripture is short, sweet, and to the point. Paul is not wasting any time in his words to the church of Thessalonica. Here we find him giving a guide for how to live a holy life.

Paul's three steps can make a huge difference in our day-to-day lives when it comes to anxiety. By focusing on rejoicing, praying, and giving thanks in all circumstances, we won't have time to think on the things making us anxious. This model is something you can lean on as you move into new phases of life. Your college years and adulthood will thank you if you make this plan a habit *now*.

Rejoice always, even in the not-so-fun situations. This doesn't mean you will avoid difficult circumstances, but it will help you not to live in panic mode. By looking for the good, you'll find it. Having a heart and mind searching for ways to enjoy life guards against the negatives that will only weigh you down.

Pray continually. Did you know you can talk to God all day? You don't have to wait to be with your parents or at church. You can be sitting at your desk at school and a thought can cause your heart to race. You can talk to God in the moment, asking Him to help you take deep breaths and think about something else. Even while you are with friends in a compromising situation, you can cry out to God in your head for a way out.

Give thanks. We don't have to wait for Turkey Day to acknowledge the blessings all around us. An attitude of gratitude is a powerful resource. When we are willfully thinking about what we have to be thankful for, it puts a protective wall between us and Anxiety

Elephants. They won't be able to break through the power of a heavenly weapon.

Rejoicing, praying, thanksgiving. These are three basic steps we can take to make a powerful change in our life.

THE NEXT SMALL STEP

Challenge yourself to see the good today, even in hard things. Find moments to pray quietly in your head. Put gratitude into action. Journal what this was like for you.

PRAYER

Dear God, help me to create a habit of rejoicing, praying, and giving thanks every day. I want to live this way to bring about a change in my life that will glorify You.

JOURNAL

....

....

....

....

....

....

....

....

....

FORTY-THREE

"Do not conform to the pattern of this world, but be transformed by the renewing of your mind."

Romans 12:2a, NIV

The world throws so many messages in your direction every day:

"Get on this social media app."

"Hang out with these people."

"Change this about yourself to be accepted."

"Don't mess up."

"Your parents will never find out."

"Hide."

"God doesn't care."

No wonder you feel the trampling of Anxiety Elephants all around you. Hearing numerous ideas can be confusing, and it is hard to distinguish between the truth and a lie when you see friends going the way the world suggests. Changing your way of living might appease the world for a moment, but it will leave you in continuous anxiety as you chase after the constantly moving goal posts.

Transforming our minds keeps us focused on the truth from God. His directives are ones we can count on to stay consistent for every generation. Allowing God's word to mold your values and beliefs doesn't make you mean or judgmental; it lets Him be the authority of your life, removing at least one role from your shoulders.

There is a series of movies out with cars and trucks transforming into robots to save the world and other realms. Villains enter the scene on a path of destruction, convincing some humans to join them as they work to eradicate those who will not bow to their ideas. The change from old cars to high-powered technology happens in a moment, and the coolest vehicles appear with personality and swag for days.

Reading God's word can bring about this type of change. Think of it like an instruction manual. As you put each step into action, it gives you the fuel and power you need to stand against your enemy. This keeps Anxiety Elephants from coming in and twisting your thoughts. When we know the truth, the confusion the world tries to throw at our security doesn't stick.

THE NEXT SMALL STEP

Grab a Bible and look up the book of Romans. You will find it in the New Testament after Acts. Find our scripture from today and underline it. Take a look at Genesis to see how creation began. Discover the family tree of Jesus in the first verses of Matthew (also in the New Testament). Let God's word come alive right before your eyes!

PRAYER

Thank You, God, for Your powerful word. Help me to fall in love with its truth.

JOURNAL

....

....

....

....

....

FORTY-FOUR

"Therefore put on the full armor of God, so that when the day of evil comes, you may be able to stand your ground, and after you have done everything, to stand."

Ephesians 6:13, NIV

I always loved riding four-wheelers with my cousin in the summer. It was the closest thing we could get to driving for a couple more years. She was much more willing to go on adventures than most of the people in my life, allowing me to experience fun I would have missed. One day, we decided to go down a different trail leading to a steeper hill. We almost made it. We got to the top but didn't have enough power to get the back wheels off the rock and onto the road. We flipped backwards into the stone and dirt holding our tire tracks. Luckily, we were not hurt traveling in reverse down this slope. Our helmets protected us from what could have been a dangerous situation.

Why does a soldier wear armor? That's right—to protect themselves in battle against injury.

God gave us this direction to put on armor for the same reason. One important piece is the helmet. We wear physical helmets for all sorts of activities—baseball, softball, horseback riding, riding bikes, etc. If you fall or get hit in the head, this piece of equipment protects you from serious injury just like it did for me and my cousin.

The helmet of salvation does the same for us. It protects our minds from hurtful thoughts that could cause us serious pain. This helmet also gives us protection against the devil, our spiritual enemy, who plots and lays traps to trip us up. When we put this helmet on regularly, we are suiting up to guard ourselves against his schemes, and God's wisdom is provided to us so we can stand strong.

What is the helmet of salvation? This is our relationship with Christ. Having salvation in Him gives us the confidence we need to stand firm against Anxiety Elephants. Putting on this daily protection— that we are secure in Christ—reminds us that our enemies can't take us away from our Heavenly Father.

THE NEXT SMALL STEP

Look up Ephesians 6:10-17. Write down every piece of armor Paul tells us to wear daily. Remember, God has given you these items of protection to stand courageous!

PRAYER

Dear Jesus, thank You for the helmet of salvation to stand firm against all evil schemes set against me.

JOURNAL

....

....

....

....

....

....

....

....

....

FORTY-FIVE

"Jesus Christ is the same yesterday and today and forever."

Hebrews 13:8, NIV

I have come to love roller coasters! As a family, we would rather vacation to a place with thrills and loops instead of a beach with quiet. We cannot get enough of the adrenaline rush when the coaster takes off from zero to sixty in seconds. However, there is one type of ride I will almost always refuse to get on . . . drop towers.

If I am going to ride, I need it to have a track leading up somewhere and not stopping in the downward motion. My husband did get me on a ride like this once. His last statement to me was, "Oh, it only drops you one time." After the fourth drop and thinking we were going to die, I did let out a laugh while shedding a tear. The high school boys behind me got the best laugh of the day.

This drop ride had different sequences, so you never knew what to expect when you got on it. Constant change leaves you with great anxiety, wondering what your experience will be. Anxiety on this ride feels much like the anxiety we face in the real world.

You never know when it will come, what it will feel like, or how far it will drop you. The repeat sequence may come immediately or weeks down the road. The lack of steadiness in a turbulent life—this is exhausting.

Jesus provides us with the consistent companion we need to exit this ride. He is a steady force that guides our steps with security and direction that has stood the test of time. What He provided for many on the pages in our hands, He will do for us. He is a constant source of peace, love, and calmness when we look to Him.

His presence never shuts down or needs repairing. Stay connected to the One who is always reliable, always there, and already present in the future.

THE NEXT SMALL STEP

Write a good-bye letter to your anxiety roller coaster. It's time to skip the next ride.

PRAYER

Thank You, God, for getting me off the roller coaster ride of anxiety and being my steady foundation.

JOURNAL

....

....

....

....

....

....

....

....

....

....

FORTY-SIX

"Even though I walk through the darkest valley,
I will fear no evil, for you are with me; your
rod and your staff, they comfort me."

Psalm 23:4, NIV

We had just seen him. He was cracking jokes at P.E. and making the English teacher roll her eyes while smiling at another one of his stories. The bell rang, backpacks were zipped, and buses were loaded. Everyone said their "see you tomorrow."

Tomorrow arrived without our friend. He was gone. The eighth-grade hall was filled with sobs instead of laughter. Youth pastors, counselors, and teachers were all ready and willing to hear every student's questions or to sit in silence. All we had to do was go where they waited.

For a time, I chose to walk through this dark valley alone. I pretended like I didn't need to talk through the heartache I felt. My prayers were even filled with lies. Not allowing the Good Shepherd to guide me with His staff caused me to live in constant fear of car wrecks or other terrible situations happening. I finally realized I could not navigate this dark valley without God's leading.

When shepherds are guiding their sheep on a dangerous path, they use their staff and gently put pressure on the sheep to keep it going in the right direction. This allows the sheep to sense the presence of their shepherd and know they are safe and not alone.

God was with me during this dark time, and He is with you. His presence will bring you comfort, and He will help you to continue forward on this journey. He tenderly moves you along, much like the shepherd moves his flock.

THE NEXT SMALL STEP

Did today's text trigger a thought to a dark valley you have
tried to walk alone? Write it out as a prayer of surrender.
God's staff will tenderly guide you through this step.

PRAYER

*Thank You, God, for guiding me on this path. Even
when it is dark, I know I can trust You.*

JOURNAL

....

....

....

....

....

....

....

....

....

....

....

....

FORTY-SEVEN

"...He said to them, 'Let the little children come
to me, and do not hinder them, for the kingdom
of God belongs to such as these.' "

Mark 10:14, NIV

If Jesus was sitting face-to-face with you right now, what would you tell Him about your anxiety?

Have you ever thought about it? How would the conversation go if Jesus was hanging out in your room eating popcorn, drinking soda, and watching funny cat videos with you? Would you cry or pour out frustration? Would you ask Him how to make it all stop? Would you sit in silence, somehow feeling peace just being in His presence?

When Anxiety Elephants invade, they work hard to convince you to find a place to hide. It can be easy for us to believe no one will listen because they have better things to do. The words "Don't bother them" run through your mind a million times.

We may not be sharing our favorite snack foods with Jesus, but He wants you to come to Him exactly like the scenario above ... crumbs on your fingers and tears in your eyes. You are not aggravating Him when you need to spew out your inner turmoil.

Jesus specifically says to let the youth—you guys—come to Him. He says to not hinder or stop you. He doesn't want any person or anything, even Anxiety Elephants, to stop you from coming to Him. He looks at you with wonder in His eyes ready to take hold of everything you lay at His feet.

As you begin to talk to Jesus, He opens His arms and pulls you close. When your words are finished, it's His turn. Your Savior and Friend pours out life-giving statements where anxiety once dwelled. Grace and mercy fill your heart as He restores your soul.

THE NEXT SMALL STEP

Now that we have painted a picture of you hanging out with Jesus, talking about all the things, give it a try. If it helps, grab a snack and pull up an empty chair.

PRAYER

Jesus, I never imagined talking to You like we were hanging out in my room, but I like it. It reminds me that You want this type of close relationship with me. Thank You for loving me in such a big way.

JOURNAL

....

....

....

....

....

....

....

....

....

....

FORTY-EIGHT

". . . We do not know what to do, but our eyes are on you."

2 Chronicles 20:12b, NIV

There are times you just don't know what to do when the anxiety attack comes. You try everything you have used in the past and nothing works. It feels worse. The attack is coming from all sides.

King Jehoshaphat experienced a battle raging physically around him much like you may be going through internally. He was getting bombarded by three enemies closing in on him at the same time. They had come to wage war and bring destruction to the king and his people. The element of surprise allowed the enemy troops to get over halfway to Jerusalem before Jehoshaphat knew what was happening. He was alarmed and did not know what to do, how to respond, or where to send troops. For him, the only choice was to stop and seek the Lord.

As Jehoshaphat waited, God gave His direction through the Levite priest, Jahaziel. The Lord delivered peace and encouragement when He told them not to be afraid of the vast army, for the battle was His (verse 15). The next day, the king sent out worshippers ahead of the army. Before the soldiers could go out in their armor, praise of God's faithfulness was sent up first through the singers. Can I be honest and say I'm not sure how I would feel about grabbing my tambourine and going ahead of the shields? But they had faith God would be true to His promise. We can believe the same.

As they were rejoicing, God was ambushing the enemy.

When we turn our eyes to God in anxious moments and choose to worship Him, our focus moves from what is causing us anxiety to the One who is greater than our Anxiety Elephant enemy. Instead of looking at the problem, we look to the Problem Solver. We can use our praise just as King Jehoshaphat did before the battle, in the battle, and when the battle was won.

What are some of your favorite worship songs right now? Use these anthems of praise as your battle cry against Anxiety Elephants.

THE NEXT SMALL STEP

Make a worship battle playlist to listen to when
the anxiety is attacking from all sides.

PRAYER

*You are worthy of my praise, Lord! Just as You were faithful
to King Jehoshaphat, I know You will do the same for me.*

JOURNAL

....

....

....

....

....

....

....

....

....

FORTY-NINE

"For he has not despised or scorned the suffering
of the afflicted one; he has not hidden his face
from him but has listened to his cry for help."

Psalm 22:24, NIV

In all my conflict with anxiety, I wondered if God was there with
me and if He could hear my cries. I felt exhausted and alone. My
thoughts and mind stayed in the same pattern 24/7. I couldn't find
the strength to get up and out from under Anxiety Elephants.

Have you found yourself in this place with anxiety? Have you wondered if God hears your plea anymore? Have you thought of yourself
as undeserving of help—especially His?

At this point in the journey, you may need to make a turn, an about-
face from the direction you are going. Our Abba Father does not de-
spise us or our afflictions. He doesn't view you as unfit, nor is He ignoring your appeal for help. If you are ready to make a mental shift
and hear from Him, it is time to begin the cleaning-out process.

How does this cleaning-out process work? What do you need to do
to get the mud and muck out of your mind to see that God is not
hiding, but instead, that He is your place of refuge to bring every
hardship?

Pull back the mask of *I'm fine* and acknowledge the truth. You are
not okay and that is okay with Him. Recognizing this gives Jesus
room to do the work only He can do. Going to church helps in this
cleaning-out process. Being with a body of believers will strengthen
you. Experiencing the power of the Holy Spirit through worship and
hearing God's word washes your soul.

This is a powerful part of your next steps in this journey. You have pressed down your troubles for far too long. By holding on to so much, there is no space available for you to hear or feel God. Maybe you didn't realize how tight your grip has become on the anxiety trying to grip you. It is time to release it all.

THE NEXT SMALL STEP

Write all your troubles below. It's time to let them go.

PRAYER

Thank You, God, for allowing me to share my afflictions with You. Knowing You don't turn Your head from me when I need You most gives me the extra push I need to change direction.

JOURNAL

....

....

....

....

....

....

....

....

....

FIFTY

"Anxiety weighs down the heart, but a kind word cheers it up."

Proverbs 12:25, NIV

Anxiety is so overwhelming, you can't breathe. What breath you do get out is very shallow. It can be crippling. It keeps you from enjoying your life and living it to the fullest. Trying to hide the pain only gives anxiety more power.

Honestly, I thought my superpower was being able to keep everything bottled up and deal with it alone. My solo struggle was actually more like kryptonite.

The closer you hold anxiety to your heart, the more power you give it. It weakens you, crushing you little by little. Anxiety wants to isolate you because it knows if you are not around anyone else, no support or encouragement can be spoken over you.

There are times Anxiety Elephants lead you into a place of isolation and drag you down a dark path of despair. Depression can sometimes be a comrade to anxiety. Battling the two together often feels difficult to defeat. I remember. But there is a way out.

The first step to getting out from under isolation is to verbally confess the pain you are carrying and your efforts to try and fix it alone. Second, after confessing and receiving God's forgiveness, you must forgive yourself. If God can forgive you and cast the weight of guilt far, far away, you can do the same.

Third, start rebuilding your community. Maybe you have pushed friends away and closed yourself off. If so, it is time to relearn how to have friends and how to be a friend. Allow mentors back in who spoke life into dead places.

Prayer is the most crucial step. You don't have to wait for someone to ask if you need prayer. You are not bothering people by requesting prayer. Family and friends love you, and you matter to them. Prayer changes things, sweet friend, and it's time for things to change.

THE NEXT SMALL STEP

Text a friend or mentor to ask for prayer about
anything you are facing right now.

PRAYER

Jesus, show me the people You have prepared to be in my community of support. If You trust them to be in my life, so can I.

JOURNAL

....

....

....

....

....

....

....

....

....

FIFTY-ONE

"But he said to me, 'My grace is sufficient for you,
for my power is made perfect in weakness.' "

2 Corinthians 12:9a, NIV

I am not enough.

How could I allow myself to feel and act this way?

Why am I not trusting God?

I am a disappointment to God and to those around me.

Have you ever had ungracious thoughts about yourself? The list above includes things I spoke over myself daily. I woke up with persecuting statements and would go to bed repeating the same accusations. I was so afraid of failure that I saw perfection as my only option. Grace wasn't for someone like me—or so I thought.

Praise God, I was wrong.

Today's message is for all the perfectionists out there. I know what it's like to read devotionals and put the pressure on to get it right every single time. Or to walk the halls of school overly prepared for every class, anxiously waiting to be called on with the correct answer on the tip of the tongue. Even getting up in the morning smiling when sleep is a stranger, so no one thinks you are ever grumpy. When the goal of perfection is not reached, what happens? Do you want to give up? The enemy is good at making us feel like we will never meet our own standard.

God wants you to know He has grace for you. He wants you to see yourself the way He sees you. He sees His child who desperately wants to move forward.

Instead of looking at where you are not, take a look back and see where you once were. Consider how far you've come. He will love you through this journey and get you to where He wants to take you. He has not given up on you, so don't give up on yourself.

THE NEXT SMALL STEP

Write down areas where you have unrealistic expectations and how you can begin to give grace to yourself.

PRAYER

Thank You, God, for Your amazing grace. Help me to allow that grace to wash over me.

JOURNAL

....

....

....

....

....

....

....

....

....

....

FIFTY-TWO

"So I say, walk by the Spirit, and you will
not gratify the desires of the flesh."

Galatians 5:16, NIV

"You are the most beautiful girl I have ever seen." Fifteen-year-old me stood frozen with my cheese plate at a wedding in the mountains the first time a boy ever said those words to me. I didn't appreciate how much courage it took for him to come up to me not knowing if rejection waited for him on the other side of his compliment. But, because he fled the scene, I never got an opportunity to know his name.

As the dating years begin, anxious thoughts and feelings multiply when you find yourself around the opposite sex. Those you used to view in the friend zone are now looking dateable. But do they want to date you? What if they say no? How do you even have normal conversations now with all these scenarios playing out in your mind? How do you stand firm on what God tells you to do when the pressure comes to go a little further?

When you are walking in a relationship with the Lord, He will help you through this awkward season. There is no getting around the extra flutter in your heart, but spending time with God equips you with knowledge on how to connect in new relationships without blurring lines you know do not need to be crossed.

Even though the boy with the long hair panicked and ran off, my boy-band husband did not. He did forget my name and almost choked when he realized I knew his ex-girlfriend, but he did not allow anxious thoughts and the fear of rejection stop him from pursuing me . . . well, he almost did, but that's another story for another book! Setting boundaries helped us not put ourselves in compromising situations that would be detrimental to our relationship. Keeping our walk with God top priority allowed those parameters to halt anxious feelings from taking over.

Walking by His direction is for your protection in every relationship.

THE NEXT SMALL STEP

Ask your parents about the first date they ever had.

PRAYER

God, this dating stuff is uncomfortable. Help me to stand firm within the boundaries You give me. I know they are for my own good.

JOURNAL

....

....

....

....

....

....

....

....

....

....

FIFTY-THREE

"When anxiety was great within me, your
consolation brought me joy."

Psalm 94:19, NIV

Anxiety does not wait for you to prepare before dealing out an attack. It wants to be superior in your mind and heart, using crushing blows to overpower you. Anxiety Elephants trample in, overtaking your life and making you feel beat-up and defeated. I cannot count the number of times an onslaught of battles would come as I put my hands on the steering wheel. Driving down the road with eighteen-wheelers speeding past me in the fast lane always pushed my search for an exit much sooner than needed. Not being able breathe made the side of the road my safe place until the torture was over. Comfort in those times seemed so far away.

I decided to look up the definition of "consolation" in today's verse. Merriam-Webster's dictionary tells us it means "the act or an instance of consoling . . . comfort."[4] So our verse is telling us that when the feeling of anxiety is great, God's *comfort* will bring us joy.

Notice the writer of this psalm says, "When *anxiety was great within me.*" He did not say "if." He is showing us that anxious thoughts *will* come after us. Thoughts of sorrow, pain, worry, conflict, doubt, and fear.

I totally get it. I know what it is like when Anxiety Elephants appear stronger than we are. I know how it feels when they paralyze you and you can literally do nothing.

BUT I also know the other side—something I desperately want you to know too—which is to feel God's comfort and His loving arms wrapped around you. He is a loving Father. It may be scary for you to turn towards His open arms, but His caring hugs bring your soul such delight when you run into His loving embrace.

At times, I put a wall up against His support because I didn't think I deserved it. Thankfully, God does not give us what we deserve. He gives us what He longs for us to have, and that is communion with Him. Don't resist His comfort and joy today. He loves you. The satisfaction you will find in His care will beat back any Anxiety Elephant coming after you.

THE NEXT SMALL STEP

Sit and let God love you. This may take a few extra
minutes to allow His comfort to comfort your weary
heart and mind. His hug is ready for you.

PRAYER

*Dear Heavenly Father, I want to feel Your comfort and joy
when the anxiety seems unbearable. I'm taking the wall
down and choosing to run towards your open arms.*

JOURNAL

....

....

....

....

....

....

FIFTY-FOUR

"See, I am doing a new thing! Now it springs
up; do you not perceive it?"

Isaiah 43:19a, NIV

Change can be painful, right? It pulls you out of the comfort zone
you have built and spent time on over the years. It puts you in places
you are not used to which can cause anxiousness, making you feel
as though you are out of control. Change makes you uncomfortable.

But . . .

Change grows you in your faith. Change in mental thought patterns
brings new clarity. Change in how you respond to situations reveals
a new confidence to reject the flesh and instead to surrender to the
guide of the Holy Spirit. Change is needed to experience the new
things God has for you.

What change are you facing? Are you fighting it because you don't
understand why the struggle is present or what God is doing? He
wants to use change to pull you in, encouraging you to lean on His
word and walk in His presence in a way you haven't before. This
change the Lord has brought about in your mind to bring a river to
the dry places where you feel mentally drained and exhausted. Even
though this change came out of nowhere, His ways are best, and you
can trust Him.

Changes you are making will continue to help you walk by faith. Sit
before the Lord and ask God what He wants you to see from this new
change.

THE NEXT SMALL STEP

Change one thing you do in the morning to keep
walking in a new way of living. Share with a parent
or close friend to hold you accountable.

PRAYER

Lord, I know I need to make some changes and I need help.

JOURNAL

....

....

....

....

....

....

....

....

....

....

....

FIFTY-FIVE

"Then God blessed the seventh day and made it holy, because on it he rested from all the work of creating that he had done."

Genesis 2:3, NIV

Busy has become a badge of honor adults wear proudly around their necks. We fill every waking minute with work to get ahead or to not fall too far behind. When downtime arrives in a blank schedule, we panic. Our brains have been trained to not slow down so we freak out when a free day pops in unexpectedly.

Chasing after temporary things is not a healthy picture we have painted for you. Instead of having your summers off with a vacation or camp sprinkled in, you now have early morning workouts, travel sports, ACT prep, and a job if time allows. School rolls around and the only difference in this setup is homework as the icing on the cake.

This is a learned habit to fill your mind and time with busyness instead of leaving space to process and rest mentally. An overactive brain eventually arrives to breakdown and burnout.

Have you found yourself in this space of exhaustion? Drum roll please . . .

Today, I officially give you permission to REST.

Busy is not the standard God gave us to follow. We have convinced ourselves that rest is a bad thing. We have put rest and laziness into the same category. But they are not the same at all. To be lazy is to avoid work or to be unwilling to work.

Resting, on the other hand, is giving yourself a moment—some time to relax and recover. Rest is needed to do the good works God created you to do. Rest allows your brain to get out of overdrive, which is where Anxiety Elephants find an open door to come in and disrupt your life.

Anxiety Elephants use busyness to overwhelm you and make you think you are being lazy if you aren't active with all the things—and I mean ALL the things. The Anxiety Elephants have convinced us we are doing something wrong if we have any free time. But when God rested, He stopped. He was still. In stillness, He was able to look at all He had done, and He saw it was good. When we rest, we follow His example.

THE NEXT SMALL STEP

The best rest comes when we disconnect. Pick one
thing to disconnect from today. Turning off your phone,
logging off social media, or saying no to an extra
activity will make you feel like a new person!

PRAYER

*Lord, I realize busy is not healthy. Help me to follow
Your example and leave room for restoring rest.*

JOURNAL

....

....

....

....

....

FIFTY-SIX

"About midnight Paul and Silas were praying and singing
hymns to God, and the prisoners were listening to them.
Suddenly there was such a violent earthquake that the
foundations of the prison were shaken. At once all the prison
doors flew open, and everyone's chains came loose."

Acts 16:25-26, NIV

Anxiety Elephants (a weapon of Satan) know the power of worship.
Our adversary attacks our thoughts to strip the weapon of worship
from our hands. Satan knows praise brings breakthrough, walls fall,
victory happens, and the salvation of others can result.

Have you tried to tell Anxiety Elephants to leave you alone, only to
have the enemy attack harder? Have you ever felt like this constant
restlessness confined you with invisible chains? Paul and Silas were
tossed into a dark place, much like the darkness we experience when
anxiety casts a shadow over our lives. The two men could have sat in
their shackles and darkness silenced by fear, but they chose to pray
and sing to the Lord. This knocked the walls of their cell down—and
the walls of everyone around them collapsed.

I can only speculate that they were hurting and sore from the thrash-
ing they took before being thrown into jail, but their focus was on
WHO had more power than the bars imprisoning them. If Anxiety Elephants have beaten you up pretty good, you may feel fairly bruised
yourself. But God is more powerful than anything Anxiety Elephants
may have thrown at you. When you choose to worship Him not only
when the sun is shining but when midnight surrounds you, His power will shake the hold of your enemy. He won't leave you alone in
that scary place. Your voice of surrender will break you free. Don't
wait for a Sunday to lift up His name.

THE NEXT SMALL STEP

Choose a worship song. When you open your mouth in faith
and worship the King of Kings, the earth will move. Your enemy
will shake when you sing in spite of your circumstances.

PRAYER

*Almighty God, You are worthy of my praise morning, noon,
and night. No matter my circumstance I will praise You.*

JOURNAL

....

....

....

....

....

....

....

....

....

....

....

FIFTY-SEVEN

"Yet it was good of you to share in my troubles."

Philippians 4:14, NIV

If you came to me with a broken arm, what would you think if I told you to wrap it up in a practice jersey and continue on with the competition you are participating in? Or what if you were having an asthma attack and my advice was to pray through it while the inhaler is sitting in my unzipped bag? You would probably look at me funny, wondering why I wouldn't get you help. This is what we are doing when we hide the mental struggle of anxiety. Just like covering up a broken bone doesn't make it go away, camouflaging anxiety doesn't fix the issue.

Multiple people helped me through my struggle with anxiety. It was intimidating to tell them at first. I wasn't sure how they would respond, considering I was not very compassionate when others came to me with their own mental battles. I didn't understand the turmoil they faced until I found myself in the same conflict. Thankfully, there was no judgment as I began to open up. They often reminded me of how much they loved me and that they were there for me.

They all shared in my troubles in different ways. Many of my friends felt relief when I talked to them about Anxiety Elephants because they had their own. Two words brought us closer together: "me too." We could stop pretending everything was okay around each other when it wasn't.

Professional counseling and speaking with my doctor brought me great comfort and support. They showed me how to dig up the causes of my struggle. In getting this kind of support, I was able to release the troubles I'd held in for so long. Without their help, I would have stayed stuck in the same harmful patterns. Just as seeking professional help for physical problems in our lives benefits us, doing so for our mental health is also important.

God is not upset with you for having all sorts of helpers in your life. He gifted them with the ability to serve you in this way. As our scripture reminds us, sharing the load is a good thing.

THE NEXT SMALL STEP

Have an open conversation about counseling with your parents.

PRAYER

I no longer want to hide my struggle with anxiety.
God, help me to talk to those who can help.

JOURNAL

....

....

....

....

....

....

....

....

....

FIFTY-EIGHT

"Have I not commanded you? Be strong and courageous.
Do not be afraid; do not be discouraged, for the Lord
your God will be with you wherever you go."

Joshua 1:9, NIV

Joshua was a mighty warrior. God instructed Moses to appoint him as the next leader of the Israelites before Moses died. Joshua was one of the twelve spies who went into the land of Canaan, the Promised Land, and reported that it was a land flowing with milk and honey. He and Caleb were the only two who faithfully believed God would deliver this land into their hands. Because of their faith, they were the only ones from their generation to enter the Promised Land. The rest of the descendants God delivered from the hands of Pharaoh and out of Egypt—including Moses—died in the wilderness.

Joshua needed mental reminders from God. This was not a time to be consumed with doubt or fear. Joshua had been called to lead these people forward. It was going to take fighting inward and physical battles and facing giant enemies to step foot into the Promised Land.

We are only nine verses into this first chapter of Joshua. This is the third time God tells him to be strong and courageous. He wants Joshua to be this way physically, but more importantly, mentally. Joshua needed to be firm in his faith over thoughts of doubt.

Anxiety Elephants will use a seed of doubt to stir a panicked moment in your heart. It grows and moves into your actions, causing your legs to feel like deadweight. The rushing adrenaline needs an outlet, but you don't know how to step forward.

Joshua had put one foot in front of the other by keeping his thoughts grounded in faith. He refused to allow negative voices to cause confusion in his mind. He focused the adrenaline running through his veins into action by marching forward instead of being frozen in fear.

THE NEXT SMALL STEP

When you feel a nervous rush, take action. Run in place, do jumping jacks, or go for a walk. In those moments, let the adrenaline burn outwardly while your thoughts grow strong on the Lord inwardly.

PRAYER

I am choosing to focus my thoughts on You today, Lord, and to move forward, no longer stuck in fear. You will give me strength and courage to continue on!

JOURNAL

....

....

....

....

....

....

....

....

....

....

FIFTY-NINE

"So God created mankind in his own image, in the image of God he created them; male and female he created them."

Genesis 1:27, NIV

I had questions and doubts about how God created me. I wondered if I was a mistake. Neither one of my siblings had a physical disability and my friends walked around with typical teenage bodies. My thoughts around my body image due to cerebral palsy caused me to isolate at times because I felt different. I allowed the enemy to use my physical appearance to define my value and worth.

As I began to bring my concerns before the Lord, He reminded me that my disability did not get to define my ability. Jesus met me in my uncertainty. He did not condemn me or throw legalistic rules in my face. Even though I could not grasp the "why" behind my impairment, I could trust that God would not bail on me.

You are not alone if you have skepticism about how God created you. The world uses people and platforms to cripple your thinking and push the message that if you have questions, maybe there is a mistake about you and your body. It tries to conceal the reality that a majority of teenagers do not feel comfortable in their skin. Hormones rage, height and weight fluctuate, voices change, and your ability to achieve or not achieve a level of success is magnified.

I know not everyone has the best homelife reading this. For some of you, it is very possible that those who said they loved you left you over physical attributes or because you wouldn't change your value system. Just as God had zero plans to abandon me, His treatment will be the same towards you.

You do not have to change who you are to be loved and approved by God. He did the accepting by creating you in His image. Coded into every cell of your DNA are unique attributes of God as He molded you together biologically and spiritually.

He did not get it wrong or make a mistake when it was your turn to be birthed into this world.

THE NEXT SMALL STEP

Ask the Holy Spirit to remind you of the truth in scripture if Satan tries to plant seeds of doubt about your God-defined identity. If you have a non-believing friend struggling in this area, write down their name and pray for their salvation so God can reveal new truth to them.

PRAYER

God, Satan is using people and technology to cause doubt in who we are. Help me to hold on to the truth of Your word. You did not make a mistake in creating me.

JOURNAL

....

....

....

....

....

....

....

....

SIXTY

"Though one may be overpowered, two can defend themselves. A cord of three strands is not quickly broken."

Ecclesiastes 4:12, NIV

I was speaking at a local elementary school a few years ago about anxiety. After I shared my story and we practiced some coping skills together, the courage of a third-grade boy still stands out. In front of the entire group, he asked, "Can you tell me how to deal with social anxiety?"

I was speechless.

If this third grader was struggling with social interactions, God brought to my attention how hard it can be for teens like you. He also reminded me of being a teenager and stumbling my way through the awkward first group dates and school events. I am still wiping the blue eye shadow away and shaking my head at the athletic socks and Jesus sandals I wore for my first homecoming dance.

Opportunities are coming your way to go to parties, school dances, dates, group outings, concerts, and the list could go on. You want to go, but you get a little nauseated mixed with dizzy just thinking about leaving your room—in other words, your comfort zone.

If you are honest, you are afraid to be around others because rejection may follow you. Worst-case scenarios play through your mind, causing you to doubt that anyone really wants you there. What if you say something silly or you don't know anyone else? What if they laugh and make fun of you but escaping is not an option? What if you don't get invited back after you go? Rather than risking it, you say no to everything followed by a well-thought-out excuse.

Start with baby steps. First, pick a couple of fun group outings to say yes to. When an event comes up, talk to your friends. Find out who is going and plan to arrive together. Set a time limit so you don't feel pressured to stay the entire time. If you realize you are enjoying yourself, contact your parents and ask to stay a little longer.

Don't allow Anxiety Elephants to keep you from enjoying time with friends. God wants you to do life together.

THE NEXT SMALL STEP

What is the next fun event coming up you can attend with friends? From a basketball game to a bowling birthday party, write it down below with the date. Come back to this page and document how it went.

PRAYER

God, give me the courage to start doing fun things with my friends.

JOURNAL

....

....

....

....

....

....

....

....

SIXTY-ONE

"The name of the Lord is a fortified tower;
the righteous run to it and are safe."

Proverbs 18:10, NIV

When my parents called me by my first and middle name, I knew they meant business. When the last name came into play, trouble was coming. Do your parents ever call you by multiple names or even nicknames and you know what they mean by each?

God has different names too. These names give us a description of His unwavering character. Each one is a reminder of WHO He is in our life and why we can trust Him.

God is:

El Shaddai—The Lord God Almighty (Genesis 17:1)

Jehovah Shammah—The Lord Is There (Ezekiel 48:35)

Jehovah Jireh—The Lord Will Provide (Genesis 22:14)

Jehovah Shalom—The Lord Is Peace (Judges 6:24)

Immanuel—God with Us (Matthew 1:23)

Friend—Friend of Sinners (Matthew 11:19)

Yahweh—Lord, Jehovah (Genesis 2:4)

El Roi—The God Who Sees Me (Genesis 16:13)

Advocate—We have an Advocate with the Father, Jesus Christ the Righteous One (1 John 2:1)

Comforter—Our Comforter in sorrow when our hearts are faint (Jeremiah 8:18)

Wonderful Counselor—He will be called Wonderful Counselor (Isaiah 9:6)

When you feel Anxiety Elephants closing in, call God by any of His names and He will be a strong tower. He will be a safe place to run to where you don't get trampled.

THE NEXT SMALL STEP

Do a quick internet search for names of God. Write new ones you discover below. When you cry out, He will be listening.

PRAYER

God, thank You that I can call Your name using any description of truth and You are listening to me.

JOURNAL

....

....

....

....

....

....

....

....

....

....

SIXTY-TWO

"The Lord your God is with you, the Mighty Warrior who saves. He will take great delight in you; in his love he will no longer rebuke you, but will rejoice over you with singing."

Zephaniah 3:17, NIV

Sit and ponder today's thought-provoking verse with me. Go back and read it again and put your name everywhere you see the word *you*. Did the verse become more personal and real?

The Lord our God is in our midst. Wherever you are, He is right there with you. It could be a dark bedroom or a bathroom in the school gym. He is close by even when you are sitting in a metal chair on a Wednesday night at youth group wondering if you are alone.

"The Mighty Warrior who saves!" It may look like you will never get past Anxiety Elephants and you won't ever overcome them, but those thoughts are lies. Today's scripture shows us something different. He is more powerful than those anxious reflections. His timing may not look like ours, but He will always rescue us.

He is rejoicing over you with gladness! He feels great joy and delight in you. It doesn't matter your situation or your circumstance. Your Heavenly Father is captivated by you. He created you in His image. Everything He created, He called good—including you.

God takes it one step further and exalts over us with loud singing—not a quiet whisper. He is singing passionately and rejoicing over each and every one of us. God's singing over you doesn't stop because anxiety may come in.

Abba Father wants to quiet your anxiety with His love today.

THE NEXT SMALL STEP

Use this verse to lift your head in victory when Anxiety
Elephants wage another battle against you. Hold on
to the promise that God rejoices over YOU.

PRAYER

God, when I sit and think about You rejoicing
over me . . . delighting in me . . . wow . . .

JOURNAL

....

....

....

....

....

....

....

....

....

....

....

....

SIXTY-THREE

"The angel of the Lord came back a second
time and touched him and said, 'Get up and
eat, for the journey is too much for you.' "

1 Kings 19:7, NIV

"I have had enough, Lord . . . take my life;
I am no better than my ancestors."

1 Kings 19:4, NIV

Elijah straight up felt like dying. These are the words he spoke after making a major proclamation for God and seeing a huge victory. He boldly stood up to King Ahab and his 450 fake prophets of Baal. Elijah outran a tiny rain cloud after a three-year drought and famine. He experienced God's goodness and miracles. Now we see him running in fear and hiding from an evil woman named Jezebel.

Have you ever felt like asking God to take your life? Or have you thought about how much better people would be without you here? This is a safe place to be honest. I remember telling God at one point in my life how I was a burden and everyone around me would be better off if I weren't here. My husband and I were leading worship and active in our church, but I was crumbling under a weighty voice telling me I had nothing to offer.

Scary place to be.

God didn't allow Elijah to stay there. He helped me move out of that mental dungeon, and he doesn't want you to stay in that place either. He sent an angel to Elijah, giving him clear instructions: rest and eat. When's the last time you got a good night's sleep? Are you trying to survive off of energy drinks, or are you hydrating with a couple of liters of water a day? Can you recall the last time you ate a good meal and not one out of a drive-thru window?

These are steps you can implement physically to take care of yourself mentally.

God created your body to give you cues. When we feel anxiety welling up inside, sometimes it is because our body is trying to tell us to stop and take a break or telling us it is time to eat. What is your body telling you?

THE NEXT SMALL STEP

Have you ever said the words Elijah spoke and felt like dying? It is time to tell your parents or an adult you feel safe talking to.

PRAYER

Help me to listen to my body cues, God. You have me here for a reason and I want to live it out.

JOURNAL

....

....

....

....

....

....

....

SIXTY-FOUR

> "'For I know the plans I have for you,' declares
> the Lord, 'plans to prosper you and not to harm
> you, plans to give you hope and a future.'"
>
> Jeremiah 29:11, NIV

Notice this verse doesn't say, "I have a plan for you, as long as you don't struggle with anxiety."

I believed there was nothing I was going to be able to do with my life because the anxiety was so strong inside. Crippling thoughts in my present terrified me about my future. My anxiousness always had me scripting out catastrophes that blocked any potential for a "what might be one day."

Do you ever feel this way?

Jeremiah reminds us that God has a plan for everyone. He didn't skip us or take our plan away because Anxiety Elephants decided to show up in our lives. His plan for you involves hope and a future. His plan also involves using this anxiety for good.

Now, I get it. Trying to wrap your brain around God using something so painful for good is hard to grasp, but it is true. His plan does not include wasting a bad season, a hurtful circumstance, or unfair situations. Everything in your life He will use. The anxiousness you are experiencing doesn't change what He has in store for you. The good news is that we are not that powerful.

Your Heavenly Father can use the attacks you have felt to show compassion to a friend at school who is going through the same thing and feels all alone. God could use the anxiety you have overcome to share your story on social media and reach someone on the other side of the world with hope only found in Christ. His plan could involve you speaking out at your church about anxiety and how you've found ways to cope.

Whatever His plan is for your life, it is good. You can trust Him with your right now and your tomorrows.

THE NEXT SMALL STEP

Write one dream you have for your future.

PRAYER

God, I choose to trust You with my right now and tomorrow.

JOURNAL

....

....

....

....

....

....

....

....

....

....

SIXTY-FIVE

"Accept one another, then, just as Christ accepted
you, in order to bring praise to God."

Romans 15:7, NIV

I will never forget our elementary school track meet in the sixth grade. When my brother, my friends, and I all discovered we got to miss the entire day of school, we all tried out! Anyone else willing to participate in activities to get you out of math class? I did the high jump and 400-meter race.

Coming around the last turn of my race, my legs felt like jelly. The asphalt under my feet was hot and caused my feet to push harder than I prepared for in practice. All of a sudden, I hear a group of students chanting. To my surprise, it was my team chanting for me: "Carebear! Carebear! Carebear!" That was my nickname . . . not a very cool one for a middle schooler, but it pushed me to run harder, and I ended up placing.

My friends accepted me and loved me. They knew I was different from them physically. They cheered me on even though I limped to the finish line. At that moment, I felt like everyone else. My disability did not hold me back from experiencing joy and victory.

Having friends to encourage you in hard times makes a difference.

They will be there to listen if you need to tell them about the headaches and stomachaches you feel at night because you hear your parents yelling. A friend will love on you when you feel embarrassed because you failed a test you studied really hard for. Your friends will bring the ice cream and french fries when you go through a gut-wrenching breakup. Your buddies will cheer you on when you hit the game-winning shot with your heart pounding out of your chest.

Accepting one another in this loving way brings praise to God.

THE NEXT SMALL STEP

How can you and your friends show kindness
towards one another today?

PRAYER

*Jesus, help me to look for ways to encourage my friends
and to let them encourage me when I need it.*

JOURNAL

....

....

....

....

....

....

....

....

....

....

....

....

SIXTY-SIX

"For I am not ashamed of the gospel, because it is
the power of God that brings salvation to everyone
who believes: first to the Jew, then to the Gentile."

Romans 1:16, NIV

Right before my senior year of high school started, we had an event
in our community called Disciple Now. Youth groups from several churches gathered together for a Friday night through Sunday
morning worship weekend, praising God in powerful moments or-
chestrated by the Holy Spirit. We all left that weekend wanting other
students who missed out on those three days to feel God's presence
the same way.

A senior guy came up with an idea. His thought was for all of us to
wear t-shirts the first day of school that said, *JUST JESUS*

We were all feeling some apprehension not knowing who would
stand together with neutral shirts speaking vibrant truth. Part of the
plan was to arrive early and pray as a group. To my pleasant surprise, a sea of students showed up proclaiming the gospel in the
hallways that day.

Nervousness can consume your thoughts when you think of a friend
who needs to hear the salvation message. Anxiety Elephants stomp
in, wanting to silence the Way, Truth, and Life. Satan will use the fear
of rejection and doubt to hold you back from telling others about the
love of Jesus and what He did on the cross to forgive our sin. Satan
will try to convince us that talking about where someone will spend
eternity makes us strangers and aliens in this world.

Even though it is a scare tactic, it is true. First Peter 2:11-12 reminds us that this world is not our home, so we are strangers in it.

Our home awaits us in Heaven. Let's bring as many of our friends with us that we can.

THE NEXT SMALL STEP

Get a couple of friends together and brainstorm how you can come together to witness to those in your school. Stand together among strangers to fill your heavenly home!

PRAYER

God, I don't want to be silent about the gospel. Give me boldness to share the salvation message.

JOURNAL

....

....

....

....

....

....

....

....

....

....

SIXTY-SEVEN

"For the word of God is alive and active. Sharper
than any double-edged sword, it penetrates even
to dividing soul and spirit, joints and marrow; it
judges the thoughts and attitudes of the heart."

Hebrews 4:12, NIV

I have never seen a sword with a double edge, but I can only imagine how incredible it would look! A double-edged sword will slice through anything around it trying to attack.

The Bible is a powerful resource in the process of overcoming Anxiety Elephants. It doesn't have to sit behind a display case like ancient swords of old in museums around the world. When the enemy comes charging towards you, fight back with the truth in God's word. Truth is greater than any deceiving word, including the lies Anxiety Elephants use to hold you back.

God gave us His word as a weapon to help us push back against the negative words attacking our minds. When we focus on His message, it allows us to remember the facts.

How can you use God's word as a sword to strike down Anxiety Elephants when they attack in your mind?

Change the words you are hearing in your head by the words you see. Videos you watch, books you read, and songs you listen to can lift up or tear down. Adding worship music, scrolling past inappropriate short-form videos, and reading devotions like this one will help aid in this shift you are making.

The hurtful echoes between your ears will be silenced with the life-giving encouragement you will witness in the handbook God gave all of us thousands of years ago. The Bible. His thoughts have never changed about you nor has His word. Keep your eyes on His message that has stood the test of time. This is one sharp object you will always be allowed to touch.

THE NEXT SMALL STEP

Grab colorful paper or notebook paper with markers. Write down your favorite scriptures and tape them all over your walls.

PRAYER

Dear God, help me to remember how powerful the Bible is for my life. Help me to use this weapon and not allow it to collect dust.

JOURNAL

....

....

....

....

....

....

....

....

....

....

SIXTY-EIGHT

"Above all else, guard your heart, for
everything you do flows from it."

Proverbs 4:23, NIV

We are friends, right? We have gone through a lot together. I have shared parts of my story and I hope you have found the courage to talk about some things you have experienced. We have looked at God's word, laughed, and maybe even cried. Now comes the time where I may share something you won't like. I am going here because, as your friend, I want you to know the truth.

Something I tell teenagers when I travel and speak at schools and churches is this: I respect your thoughts and opinions. All I ask is that you would be willing to hear a different perspective. Is that fair?

Here we go . . . social media is not the best place to get direction for life. I will not tell you to get off of it completely if you are on different platforms, BUT I will ask you to consider pulling back for a moment. Staring at a screen for multiple hours a day watching others live their lives can increase anxiety.

So many confusing messages happen through video, DMs, and memes. How do you know which ones to listen to? They change constantly every day, and with all the filters you have no idea who anyone is. Social media companies are pumping messages into your heart and mind, telling you what to do to make yourself better and more accepted. Oftentimes, you leave their spaces feeling worse about yourself than before you mindlessly scrolled.

Some of you may even be experiencing the hurtful side of social media because you are being bullied through the DMs. You are sent painful videos constantly and cannot get away. While blocking these bullies is a short-term solution, it doesn't solve the pain already inflicted.

Taking a break from these platforms will ease the world's pressure crushing your heart and causing your breath to weaken. You will find you no longer compare your selfies to filtered images that change every feature of someone's face.

If social media has attacked your heart and mind, walking away from it for a season is not a defeat. It is a victory in God's eyes worth celebrating.

THE NEXT SMALL STEP

One day. Take one day off of social media and journal how it goes. If one day feels too difficult, start with one hour.

PRAYER

I am surrendering my social media to You, God. I can tell it alters how I feel about myself. I no longer want it controlling me.

JOURNAL

....

....

....

....

....

....

SIXTY-NINE

"Moses said to the Lord, 'Pardon your servant, Lord. I have never been eloquent, neither in the past nor since you have spoken to your servant. I am slow of speech and tongue.' "

Exodus 4:10, NIV

Fun fact some of you may not know. Public speaking is the number one fear of adults.[5] I thought it might be spiders, snakes, or heights. But standing in front of people staring at you, in a quiet room, being judged or graded on what you say is actually scarier for most people than being trapped in a coffin with slithery creatures.

In complete transparency, my greatest fear would have to be snakes, something you may have gathered from the intro of today's devotion!

How do you feel about standing up to speak in front of your class-mates? Do you feel your palms sweating onto your paper? Do your thoughts leave your head before you even get out of your desk? Do you try to force the words, but a stutter comes out instead? Anyone ever lock their knees and faint? It totally happens!

Moses was nervous about speaking in front of people too. He had trouble getting the words out, and it took him longer to say things through stammering syllables. God knew this about Moses, but He still commanded him to go to Pharaoh and demand the release of the Israelites.

God reminded Moses He was the One who created our mouths, and He could help him say exactly what needed to be said. God taught Moses how to speak and trust He would do the work. Moses only needed to be obedient.

When you get ready to speak in front of people, know you are not the only one who feels a little anxious. Moses has been in your shoes.

Take a good deep breath before you talk. Find a spot on the back wall right above a friendly face. Let the words flow naturally instead of at a racing pace. Practice with family or in front of a mirror. Ask God to help you speak through the nerves. The more you do it, the more your confidence will increase, and your new courage will help you get past the fright.

THE NEXT SMALL STEP

Practice giving a sixty-second speech in front of a friend or a mirror.

PRAYER

*God, just as You helped Moses, give me the
words to speak when it's time.*

JOURNAL

....

....

....

....

....

....

....

....

SEVENTY

"I have told you these things, so that in me you may
have peace. In this world you will have trouble.
But take heart! I have overcome the world."

John 16:33, NIV

If only I could tell you that your life is going to be rainbows and uni-
corns. No struggle, no pain, no bullies, no rejection, no hard things,
no more Anxiety Elephants. We will experience life like this one day
in Heaven, but here on earth, Jesus is reminding us we will have
trouble. Hiding this truth from you will not equip you with godly
strategies to use when the time comes to respond.

Trouble looks different for everyone, but for some, trouble comes
in the form of anxiety. It can block your thoughts, making it difficult
to focus on schoolwork, or cause nervousness to the point you are
afraid to be around others. It can also make your body experience
strange symptoms.

Jesus is with us in our troubles. We can have hope knowing He has
overcome the world! This means He has already won the ultimate
battle.

How do you take heart when you feel anxiety coming? You can pray
and talk to the Lord in that moment. Use this scripture to remind
yourself you are not messing up because trouble has come. Remember, you are on the winning team! Think of it like this—you
are playing softball against Anxiety Elephants and your undefeated
Team Captain, Jesus, is up to the plate. They do not win, so you can
breathe a sigh of relief.

When you experience trouble, don't forget, Jesus told us we would.
Stand up tall with your shoulders back and your head up. He chose
to fight for you, and we know He never loses.

THE NEXT SMALL STEP

Jesus can help you defeat trouble by giving you peace,
giving you courage, and even giving you creative
ideas! List below ways He has helped you defeat the
trouble anxiety has caused you this past week.

PRAYER

*Thank You for telling us the truth, Jesus, about facing troubles. I
know I won't go through them alone with You fighting for me.*

JOURNAL

....

....

....

....

....

....

....

....

....

....

....

SEVENTY-ONE

"Such confidence we have through Christ before God.
Not that we are competent in ourselves to claim anything
for ourselves, but our competence comes from God."

2 Corinthians 3:4-5, NIV

I was top five in my class academically. I served on the student council, was the class president, was the Christian Bible Club president, served on the prom committee, got straight A's, and was the assistant producer for Drama Club. If there was a title, I would seek it out. The thought of failing a test or making an 89.4 would raise my blood pressure. I thought my competence—my value—was found in all that I could do. If I wasn't holding a title or leading a club or giving a tutoring session, my anxiety would be off the charts, searching for a way to numb its pull. But sufficiency is found in *being*, not doing. It's found in being content, not performing.

Do you find yourself searching for things and performances to attach your value to?

If you are under the weight of that heavy pressure, I would love to give you a hug right now. It is so difficult to go to school constantly wondering what you have to do and how perfect your grades have to be for acceptance, not just by your peers, but by your own mind. God would not ask the requirements of you that you ask of yourself.

Stop. Step back and re-read our verse for today. You can take the pressure off. God does not expect you to perform at top level day-in-and-day-out. He wants you to be content by being in a relationship with Him. You don't have to do everything to be content. You can silence the constant "do." Release the lie that "doing" defines you. Put the pressure on God. Sit back in His presence and watch what He is able to accomplish through you. You can transfer confidence from your ability to His.

THE NEXT SMALL STEP

It's time to remove the pressure of perfection off of your grades, your activities, and not making a mistake in the choices you make. Write down which area you would like to work on first.

PRAYER

Heavenly Father, for so long I have put my value in what I can do. Help me to remember You see me as valuable not because of what I can do, but because of who You are.

JOURNAL

....

....

....

....

....

....

....

....

....

SEVENTY-TWO

"I lift up my eyes to the mountains—where does my help come from? My help comes from the Lord, the Maker of heaven and earth."

Psalm 121:1-2, NIV

In football, the quarterback can't hike, throw, catch, and block all at the same time. Each player has a role. Soccer has goalkeepers, defenders, midfielders, and strikers holding set positions for ninety minutes. Teams in all sorts of sports work together and help one another ultimately achieve the goal of victory.

Help is not a four-letter word . . . yes, I know it has four letters, but what I am trying to say is that it is not a bad word. For some reason, it gets treated this way. Our culture has applauded doing everything by yourself and not "needing" others to pitch in. It has pushed this message despite the pressure and sense of failure we feel when some of us realize we can't do it all on our own.

Our verse shows us we don't have to do life all by ourselves. Looking up allows the view to shift from seeing only what *we* can do to seeing that there are more people out there to help us than we can grasp.

Asking for HELP is one of the best things you can do to stomp out anxiety. Unlocking this secret struggle to friends and trusted adults removes the heavy load you are carrying by yourself. For example, let's say you are switching rooms and moving to the basement to finally get away from your younger brother. You have boxes full of shoes, clothing, and all the little doodads your mom makes you keep from when you were younger. How much faster would you finish if you invited your friends over for pizza and a helping hand?

The Maker of heaven and earth is ready to help. God's hands were meant to carry the biggest boxes you have been trying to drag across the floor. Your hands were designed to let them go.

THE NEXT SMALL STEP

You are not weak or doing anything wrong by using these four powerful letters: HELP. This is a challenge to put this word in action.

PRAYER

God, I am asking for HELP. It's a relief to know I'm not required to carry everything on my own.

JOURNAL

....

....

....

....

....

....

....

....

....

....

SEVENTY-THREE

"May the God of hope fill you with all joy and
peace as you trust in him, so that you may overflow
with hope by the power of the Holy Spirit."

Romans 15:13, NIV

In a strange way, I felt comfortable in anxiety, doubt, and fear. Even though the attacks were painful—after all Anxiety Elephants were stomping all over my chest—it was scarier to choose hope. It felt safer in my deep hole of discouragement versus reaching out for something I didn't think I deserved. Avoiding the adventure leading to hope allowed me a window of time to pretend as though everything was fine. Or at least, normal.

God is putting a stop sign in the middle of your avoidance journey today. He wants to not just give you enough hope but to give you an overflow. The only thing to avoid now is actual avoidance.

There may be several things causing anxiety inside you. Avoiding all the issues does not make them go away. But it does open the door for problems to grow bigger and move into other areas of your life if you continue to sidestep them.

So how do you avoid avoidance?

Avoiding avoidance can be done by being honest about where you are at the moment. Do the Anxiety Elephants make you feel scared? Are you angry or frustrated? Does the urge to run away pass through your thoughts? It is okay to say any of these things out loud. By having this starting point, you know how to move forward.

Another simple tactic is to gradually expose yourself to situations that make you nervous. It could be riding on an elevator, attending church in person and sitting on the edge, or driving your car from the house to school, eventually building up courage to tackle the interstate.

God is not avoiding you. As you go through this trial, have courage to follow His lead. By facing it head-on, you are looking the Anxiety Elephants in the eye and showing them you will no longer back down.

THE NEXT SMALL STEP

Is there a thought you have been hiding you need to confront? Has a situation been holding you hostage that you are ready to face? Write down one step you will take to stop avoiding.

PRAYER

No more avoiding, Lord. I'm ready to tell You everything.

JOURNAL

....

....

....

....

....

....

....

....

SEVENTY-FOUR

"As for me, I call to God, and the Lord saves me. Evening, morning, and noon I cry out in distress, and he hears my voice."

Psalm 55:16-17, NIV

David is the writer of this psalm. As he begins, his words are different from what we read in our verses above. David shares how his thoughts are troubling him and how anxious he feels as he finds himself surrounded by enemies. He was all alone and only God was with him.

How do you feel when you are alone? When the daily separation between when you go to school and when your family goes to work arrives, do you feel anxious being away from them? Do your thoughts go to a troubling place like David when you are separated for any amount of time from people you care about?

What can you do in those moments of separation?

Talk to your parents or guardians about the fear or sadness you experience when it is time to go to school. Be honest about the thoughts you have in your head. These thoughts may feel unnerving. You may feel anxious about a car wreck happening because a classmate recently experienced this with their family. It could be you are concerned you might be forgotten and have to find a different ride home. Being specific will help those in charge of you understand your pause before leaving.

Have a plan of what to do if your caregivers are running late or plans change at the last minute. Take a good deep breath and focus on what you want to share about your day when your ride shows up.

Cry out to the Lord, as our verse directs, any time of the day when those anxious thoughts over being away from family creep in.

THE NEXT SMALL STEP

It's important your parents or guardians know how you feel when your separation occurs. Together, decide things you can do to squelch anxious thoughts when there is distance between you and your loved ones.

PRAYER

God, thank You for reminding me that You are always with me even when I am alone.

JOURNAL

....

....

....

....

....

....

....

....

....

....

....

SEVENTY-FIVE

"Therefore go and make disciples of all nations, baptizing them in the name of the Father and of the Son and of the Holy Spirit."

Matthew 28:19, NIV

It was the first time I had ever heard the waves and stood in the deep, blue water. But only knee-deep. In my mind, the sharks swam much closer to shore. A lifelong best friend had invited me to go on her family vacation to the beach. I couldn't believe my mom was totally fine with me leaving for a week, but I didn't wait for her to change her mind! We had the best time eating chicken salad sandwiches and banana taffy and staying up way past our bedtime.

At church, we had been talking about witnessing to our friends about Jesus a few days before I hopped in the van with my friend and her family for some fun in the sun. The youth pastor handed out these square pieces of paper called tracts and encouraged us to share the good news of the gospel. My friend was not in church anywhere, so I wasn't sure if she was a Christian. I tucked this card away in my suitcase just in case.

One night, my heart started beating like a drum. I knew God wanted me to talk to my friend about Jesus and ask if she was saved. The Anxiety Elephants felt so loud in my ears. I didn't know what her answer would be or what would happen after I shared. Through the fear and anxiousness, the Holy Spirit gave me words to say. My legs were shaking by the time I was done. She didn't get mad or make me leave. A few years later, she did ask Jesus into her heart, and she lives every day with her family to bring glory to Him.

It is normal to feel anxious about sharing your faith. Not knowing what will happen can be scary. God simply asks you to go. He will take care of their response. By pushing through the rumblings, you are showing Anxiety Elephants you care more about your friend's salvation than anything they can throw at you.

THE NEXT SMALL STEP

Write down the name of a friend needing to hear the gospel. Ask God to give you courage to witness to them.

PRAYER

God, help me to share Your salvation message. Please bring my friends into a relationship with You.

JOURNAL

....

....

....

....

....

....

....

....

....

....

SEVENTY-SIX

"If we are thrown into the blazing furnace, the
God we serve is able to deliver us from it, and he
will deliver us from Your Majesty's hand."

Daniel 3:17, NIV

Shadrach, Meshach, and Abednego were close friends, and they loved God with all their hearts. Following a command to bow down and worship fake gods was not happening with them, even if it meant being killed in a fiery furnace. They trusted in the One True God. It helped knowing they had each other to go through this horrifying situation, not knowing what the outcome would be.

Can you imagine being thrown into a real fire? These three young men did get tossed into the blazing inferno. They were tied down and thrown away. It was so hot, it killed the soldiers launching them in! But a miracle happened to our young friends. Not one hair was scorched. Their clothes had no burn marks. There was no campfire smell following them around. When we roast marshmallows, we smell like smoke for days, and yet not one hint of fire remained on them. Not only were they unharmed, but Jesus physically came and stood in the fire with them! The king could not believe there were now four men walking in the fire instead of three.

Who are two friends you have that will share the fire you are going through with Anxiety Elephants? By doing life together, you can get through the hard things, knowing God is with you and will help see you through every step. It helped Shadrach, Meshach, and Abednego to have each other in the face of this scary situation.

THE NEXT SMALL STEP

It's time to have a little fun! Gather around a fire or an oven for a s'mores snack with friends. Talk and share with one another about God's faithfulness as He goes through the fire with you.

PRAYER

Thank You, Jesus, for standing in the fire with me.

JOURNAL

....

....

....

....

....

....

....

....

....

....

....

SEVENTY-SEVEN

"Consider it pure joy, my brothers and sisters, whenever
you face trials of many kinds, because you know
that the testing of your faith produces perseverance.
Let perseverance finish its work so that you may be
mature and complete, not lacking anything."

James 1:2-4, NIV

Wait a minute . . . am I really going to sit here and tell you to consider it a joy when you are battling anxiety? Not only am I going to encourage you to find the joy, but I am going to take it one step farther and tell you to embrace the anxiousness when it comes.

Now, hold up . . . I don't mean embrace it by holding it close and going back to the old way of living in secret with your mental battle. I mean embrace the moment by no longer allowing Anxiety Elephants to cause you to retreat, run, and hide.

When you stand firm in the trial, you're building up your faith muscle just like you build body muscle when you work out. When we work out, we don't start out with the heaviest weights, but if we don't start with grasping some sort of weight, we will never build up our stamina and strength to take on new weight.

When you stand strong against Anxiety Elephants, panic is replaced with endurance. You're able to sustain your breathing quicker and longer. You are able to put new strategies to work to see which ones are the best for you and which ones you need to adjust.

When you stand strong against their attacks, what they used to try no longer works. You can consider it a joy because victories are happening, and faith is growing.

View the next attack like a workout session. You might struggle through it, but when you get to the other side, you will walk out with a smile on your face knowing your faith muscle is growing and perseverance is being instilled into your mind.

THE NEXT SMALL STEP

No more retreating when anxiety comes. Stand firm, take a breath, and rejoice in the faith muscle you are building.

PRAYER

Dear God, help me remember I am an overcomer and that You encourage us to not stop but to persevere.

JOURNAL

....

....

....

....

....

....

....

....

....

....

SEVENTY-EIGHT

"He says, 'Be still, and know that I am God . . . ' "

Psalms 46:10, NIV

On Monday and Tuesday afternoons, you have ball practice. You go home to finish all your homework and study for a history test. Wednesday night is church. Thursday and Friday you have piano lessons for an hour and then head to the gym to work out with friends before going to eat chips and salsa for dinner. The weekend is here, and you have tournaments, parties, more practices, and the occasional fun outing with your family. Sunday is the day you look forward to because there is time to breathe before starting all over.

An overwhelming feeling comes over you as you think about the week ahead with school and all the activities you feel like you have to do to please others and fit in. You find yourself wanting to be so busy because the anxiety you experience seems to go away when you are going nonstop.

Anxiety Elephants thrive off of a full schedule and no room for breaks. If they can keep you moving, they can stop you from dealing with all the things really bothering you inside. All this activity is being used as a numbing agent instead of as a healthy coping plan.

The Lord is not asking you to be still to keep you away from good things. He is telling us to be still because He knows how our bodies are created. Our Creator knows the mind and body need margins.

A margin is what you see in a book. Take this one for example. Notice the words do not fill up the entire white space from top to bottom or left to right. Margins are needed to give your eyes and brain a break to process information you are reading.

We need this blank space in our lives. It allows us to experience His presence in a peaceful way. Having this newfound capacity to spend time with God will help you to navigate through life much easier.

Take a few seconds to think about what your life will be like spending more time with God and less time chained to all those extra things. He can fill your cup with so much more than anything this world has to offer.

THE NEXT SMALL STEP

What is one thing you can remove from your life
to help you be still and have margin?

PRAYER

*Dear Jesus, help me to make more space for
spending time with You in my life.*

JOURNAL

....

....

....

....

....

....

....

....

SEVENTY-NINE

"Don't let anyone look down on you because you are young, but set an example for the believers in speech, in conduct, in love, in faith and in purity."

1 Timothy 4:12, NIV

You have so much to offer this world right now. Being a world-changer is not reserved for adults only. In fact, I believe your generation will bring about greater change than mine did! Your ability to impact your community and those around you is not restricted by the anxiety you bravely face. Yes, you read the word *brave* because it is a brave task you take on to get up over and over and try again.

The cool thing is Jesus sees you as you will be, not where you are right now. Struggles don't define you, which means anxiety doesn't get the final say in who you are or what your life will look like. Jesus already defined that.

You can make a difference in others' lives. There are other teenagers facing challenging attacks from Anxiety Elephants. For some people, you may be the only one who can understand. You totally get how hard it is to let others in on what's really happening. Being a comforting voice to your peers will put a spring of endurance in their step to face it just like you. God has given you hope to share.

Maybe you feel Him gently nudging you to share your testimony at your school's Bible club or church. By standing up and talking about what is helping you overcome anxiety, you will give others the courage to attempt the same strategies.

You are prepared to set a powerful example. God will give you everything you need at just the right time. Go in faith, courage, and love. You have got this, and God's got you.

THE NEXT SMALL STEP

You can do this. Talk to a ministry leader
about sharing your testimony.

PRAYER

*Heavenly Father, empower me with courage to share the testimony
You have given me. If I can help even one person, it's worth it.*

JOURNAL

....

....

....

....

....

....

....

....

....

....

....

EIGHTY

"[A]nd all are justified freely by his grace through
the redemption that came by Christ Jesus."

Romans 3:24, NIV

Has anxiety told you that you don't deserve to come out of the crummy place it's keeping you? Thankfully, God does not give us what we deserve but instead, what He wants us to have.

He desires for you to have love, joy, peace, and His favor poured out through grace.

Grace is a gift He gave not because we deserve it or because we earned it. If you are sitting there saying to yourself, "No way I deserve this kind of favor, mercy, and grace," you would be right! God gave it freely through Jesus on the cross. Long before you and I entered this world, He knew we were going to need lots of help and forgiveness. Our Heavenly Father also wanted to give us sweet reminders of the unconditional love He has for us.

Look around you outside. How different are the trees, birds, bugs, and butterflies? God put this beauty everywhere not because He owes it to us to see it every day but because He wanted us to have something that shows the colors of His amazing love every day. This gift of creation was given to you and me to reveal how important we are to Him.

You are precious in His sight.

Looking upon His handiwork outside gives you a chance to breathe in fresh air and clear your mind. Get out of the weeds where Anxiety Elephants want to keep you. As you stare up into the blue sky with the sun beaming down, think on this gift of grace. It will never be taken away from you.

THE NEXT SMALL STEP

Grab a blanket, and depending on the weather, a jacket. Go outside and look up. Close your eyes and feel the breeze. Listen to the birds and think on God's gift of grace for you.

PRAYER

I am grateful for all the beauty You gave me to see, Lord. Thank You for grace I don't deserve.

JOURNAL

....

....

....

....

....

....

....

....

....

....

....

EIGHTY-ONE

"For we know that our old self was crucified with him
so that the body ruled by sin might be done away
with, that we should no longer be slaves to sin."

Romans 6:6, NIV

Is anxiety a sin? This question would haunt me and often send me into a deeper anxiety-filled spiral thinking about the answer. If this thought keeps you up at night, I do hope today will bring clarity.

Anxiety is not a sin, but the way we deal with it can be. There is a camp for kids some of you may have attended called CentriKid, and they give a great explanation of what sin is: "Simply put, sin is the bad stuff we do that makes God sad and separates us from Him."[6] This could be something like stealing from a store, yelling at your brother or sister, lying to a teacher, or disobeying your parents.

When Anxiety Elephants attack, we can choose to respond in a way that doesn't cause us to sin. Instead of hiding it, we can tell someone. Choosing to pray in place of worrying about future events stomps out anxious thoughts. Creating new habits, versus returning to the old ones causing us harm, will set us free from sinful behaviors.

God is not mad at you because Anxiety Elephants are harassing you. We can see from our verse that we are no longer bound to the tricky schemes those elephants use to pin us down. You are not a slave to what you have always done when the panic enters your heart and mind.

Change is hard, but it will help you to live in a free way. Some experts say it takes twenty-one days to create new habits. This is only the beginning. It took multiple days, months, and even years to get into the habits you have right now. Don't give up on the process if it takes you a while to create holy habits in your thinking and living.

THE NEXT SMALL STEP

What is one thing you want to start doing when panic tries
to enter your mind to keep you away from walking in sin?

PRAYER

*God, please help me work on new ways of
responding to anxiety with holy habits.*

JOURNAL

....

....

....

....

....

....

....

....

....

....

....

EIGHTY-TWO

"Peace I leave with you; my peace I give to you. I
do not give to you as the world gives. Do not let
your hearts be troubled and do not be afraid."

John 14:27, NIV

The world feels scary sometimes. If your parents watch the news, you may hear what is happening while you are eating your Pop Tart or protein bar before school in the morning. You arrive to practice, and your friends are talking about the bad things happening in their lives. Drama consumes your phone, the anxiety you woke up with is clogging your mind, and the last thing you feel is peace.

In fact, anxiety has robbed you of peace. This precious thing was stolen, and you want it back. You don't want to walk around nervous and on edge, afraid you might explode at any moment.

Jesus said He left peace with us, so how can we walk in it?

Have a discussion with your parents about turning the news off while you are getting ready for school and tell them the reason behind your request. Do you need to change where you hang out on social media? If you find yourself feeling frustrated, down in the dumps, or angry when you finish scrolling, this is not a place providing you calm and safety.

The most important thing you can learn is to talk to Jesus. Tell Him the troubles in your heart, and ask Him to fill those places with peace. Jesus' peace leads to trust amid crazy circumstances in a chaotic world. He is ready to hear from you any time of the day. It can be at night when sleep doesn't come or at school in the bathroom stall. No matter the time or place, Jesus is ready to meet you with peace.

THE NEXT SMALL STEP

Talk to your parents about the news you are hearing.
Ask them questions and share what troubles you
about the uncertainty of the world around you.

PRAYER

*Thank You, Jesus, for peace in troubling times. Help
me to cling to the peace only You can provide.*

JOURNAL

....

....

....

....

....

....

....

....

....

....

....

EIGHTY-THREE

"Search me, God, and know my heart; test
me and know my anxious thoughts."

Psalm 139:23 NIV

Did you know tens of thousands of thoughts enter your mind every day? These thoughts come so fast we don't even realize when they arrive. Thoughts consume our brain from TV, social media, friends, video games, teachers, parents, church, music, and ourselves.

I have a question: does a thought lead to an action or an action lead to a thought? The way I look at it is that a thought is like a seed. You water it the more you think on it, and it will eventually sprout into an action.

What do you want to think on? What does God want you to think about?

We often talk about how to honor God through our body. How we treat our bodies with the food we put in them and activities we become involved with are important. As I began to work on this devotional, it hit me: we need to acknowledge the mental aspect of glorifying God, not merely the physical.

Just as we don't eat junk all day because it would give us a stomachache, if we let all the bad thoughts in, this can cause pain through anxiety attacking us. When an anxious thought tries to enter your mind, test it.

Psalm 139:23 gives us direction on how to do this. When we ask God to search our heart and test our thoughts, He will give clarity to the anxious ones needing to go. Stop and ask yourself, "Is this thought going to honor God if I let it stay?" If the answer is no, change the words seeking entry into something bringing glory to God.

THE NEXT SMALL STEP

Let's practice. Today, instead of thinking, "What if I fail this test?", shift to "I am prepared and ready to try my best." The beauty of practice is it doesn't make you perfect—it makes you better.

PRAYER

I want my thoughts to be pleasing to You, Lord.
Help me to pay attention to what I let in today. Test
my thoughts and reveal what needs to go.

JOURNAL

....

....

....

....

....

....

....

....

....

....

....

EIGHTY-FOUR

"I no longer call you servants, because a servant does not know his master's business. Instead, I have called you friends..."

John 15:15a, NIV

Jesus was a friend to so many. There was not a list of attributes they had to hold or an application to fill out. Jesus was friends with Peter, knowing the day would come that Peter would deny ever serving with him, much less knowing him. Jesus called Judas a friend and invited him in as a disciple, knowing Judas would betray him for thirty pieces of silver. Jesus called Zacchaeus a friend even though Zacchaeus was a crooked tax collector stealing from others to line his pockets. Jesus welcomed them all.

Did you know God considers YOU a friend? How cool is that?! To know the God of the universe wants to be friends with you is kind of a big deal. You are pretty special to Him.

He wants to spend time with you and build a friendship. It's not all about rules and guidelines but getting to know Him and sharing all of you without holding back. God likes for us to bring the good, the bad, and the ugly to Him. We can come to Him as we are, in the same way we would when hanging out with friends—talking and laughing all night long. Nothing is off-limits. It is the same with the Lord. He has so much to share with you. And He wants you, as His friend, to have the freedom to share everything with Him.

Have Anxiety Elephants caused you to feel like you have to hide because there is no way God would want to be friends with someone like you who's having a hard time with something like anxiety?

God doesn't see these things in you. He sees YOU.

He loves YOU.

He believes in YOU.

He is not mad at YOU.

He called you friend, and this will never change. Allow Him to be the friend you have always wanted.

THE NEXT SMALL STEP

Invite a friend to church, then head out for a meal afterwards. As you hear God's word together, think on how Jesus calls you both a friend.

PRAYER

Thank You, God, for considering me a friend.

JOURNAL

....

....

....

....

....

....

....

....

....

EIGHTY-FIVE

"When I said, 'My foot is slipping,' your
unfailing love, Lord, supported me."

Psalm 94:18, NIV

Falling down is embarrassing, but falling down in front of people
is the absolute worst! I was walking through a store with a friend,
and they had just mopped the floors. Thankfully, I was behind her.
The caution signs were out, but I was not paying attention. We were
on a mission, so this was not a slow stroll. Suddenly, I took a big
step and my foot slipped. Somehow, I did not fall, but I could feel
the cringy look on my face as my arms flailed in the sky and my boot
heel did an interesting move under my leg. She turned around, just
as I caught myself, not knowing what had happened. Unfortunately,
the people behind me got to see it all go down.

Anxiety does this to us. We can be walking along, enjoying life, and
all of a sudden—BAM—it pulls our feet out from under us. We slip,
wondering if anyone sees what is happening. Unease consumes our
thoughts as we question what might happen next. The label of being
a failure consumes our every step.

Falling down or making a mistake does not make you a failure; it
makes you human. Jesus knew we were going to have slips and falls,
so He came to give support. This scripture reminds us, even in these
slippery moments, that the Lord has got our back.

Once you get the hang of your footing, you will recognize the slippery spots much earlier. And if you should slip, get back up, dust
yourself off, and keep walking towards your destination. A slip may
slow you down, but it won't take you out.

THE NEXT SMALL STEP

Have you ever fallen in public? Strike up a fun conversation with your family to see what embarrassing moments you have all faced. This is a reminder of the humanness you all possess.

PRAYER

You are the greatest supporter that I have, Jesus. Thank You for loving me and keeping my steps secure.

JOURNAL

EIGHTY-SIX

"And let us consider how we may spur one
another on toward love and good deeds."

Hebrews 10:24, NIV

Growing up, my friends and I loved to serve at a place called the Mission of Hope. At Christmastime, families in need would come and we would get to walk the children around to pick out new coats, shoes, and toys. They had an opportunity to go into a large room with no heat and search through used toys to see what treasures could be found among items discarded by other families. Watching their faces light up helped us to put things going on in our own lives into a new perspective.

Helping others, when you are struggling yourself, is a powerful thing. It takes the focus off whatever is hard that you are experiencing and opens the door to the love and good deeds possible in your part of the world. It brings joy to others but also to you. Inviting others to join you in doing these good deeds makes the experience even more fulfilling.

I know things may be difficult for you right now. Life is throwing you curveballs right and left. Anxiety can take over and cause you to laser focus on what you are facing and see nothing else.

How can you challenge yourself to help someone who is going through something hard themselves and needing help?

By searching for a way to do good deeds, it takes your flashlight off of your struggle and puts a spotlight on helping others. These acts will fill your soul with peace and gladness and bring a smile to God's face as you obey His word.

THE NEXT SMALL STEP

Is there a family in need around you? What about kids
in the children's ministry of your church who need a
mentor in their life? Is there a student who could really
use some friends? What is an action you and your friends
could take together to serve your community?

PRAYER

*Open my eyes to see the needs of others. I want to serve
You, God, by seeing different ways I can serve others.*

JOURNAL

....

....

....

....

....

....

....

....

....

....

EIGHTY-SEVEN

"Submit yourselves, then, to God. Resist the devil, and he will flee from you."

James 4:7, NIV

For years, my daughters begged us for a dog. We gave them the same reasons you've heard to not get a pet:

- Too much responsibility
- No one home to take care of it
- No one will play with it
- It will destroy the house
- It will eat my shoes and stain my floors

Sound familiar?

But the persistent asking finally worked. We brought home a mini goldendoodle named Cooper Hashbrown and surprised them one year a few weeks before Christmas. When they opened the box, they couldn't decide if he was real or a toy. This twenty-five-pound ball of fur thinks he is the most ferocious animal on the face of the planet. He will bark his head off, warning of danger, if you get close to him. His form of attack is to lick you to death or lay on top of your feet as he is doing while I finish typing this book.

His bark is worse than his bite.

This reminds me of our enemy, the devil. He comes at us loud, trying to intimidate us with the thud of Anxiety Elephants pushing further and further into our space. Satan wants us to think we are no match for them. He uses a megaphone to amplify his tiny voice and causes us to believe a lion is standing ready to attack.

When we submit ourselves to the Lord and defer to what He says is best, it helps us to take bold action and resist the attack of the enemy. Resisting turns us in the opposite direction of where the devil wants us to go.

Because we have God on our side, we are more powerful than the devil! His bark will never make it past God's bite.

THE NEXT SMALL STEP

When the devil tries to heave a booming voice
of worry, doubt, or fear your direction, RESIST.
Trust God, go in faith, and don't be afraid.

PRAYER

*Thank You, God, for showing me that through
You I am more powerful than my enemy!*

JOURNAL

....

....

....

....

....

....

....

....

EIGHTY-EIGHT

"Each of you should use whatever gift you have
received to serve others, as faithful stewards
of God's grace in its various forms."

1 Peter 4:10, NIV

We each have received a gift. Those gifts will shine brightest through the broken places of our lives. Where God heals us, we experience His love, grace, mercy, and forgiveness. We can serve others best through understanding where brokenness can take a person, and in turn, how God can take the person through it.

Because of the broken areas anxiety brought about in my life, I experienced healing I didn't realize I needed. I began to feel compassion the way Jesus had compassion. He gave me a gift of hope and restoration. I wanted those who battle Anxiety Elephants to know the gifts available to them. I had to share what I'd learned. God opened doors for me to do that in ways I could not have imagined.

He wants to do the same through you.

Open your gift. God is writing a shareable story through you. He didn't give this for you to keep to yourself. He gave it to you because there is someone out there who needs to hear from your experience. Your pouring into them won't look identical to others. The encouragement you have to offer might be revealed through a song, sports, or theater. God is not bound to one type of story box. Other teens may think they are the only ones who get trampled on by Anxiety Elephants. They may believe this is the way life is meant to be. There are people waiting for you to unbox your gift. Remember, it won't look like anyone else's. This is God's unique way of putting His one story—the gospel—to use in multifaceted ways. If He doesn't put you in one certain box, stop doing it to yourself. Share what you have, as He continues to write.

THE NEXT SMALL STEP

Share your gift—your story. Write it here first to help you.

PRAYER

Give me the courage to share my story, Lord. Thank You for giving me hope. Help me to share with others who are searching.

JOURNAL

....

....

....

....

....

....

....

....

....

....

....

....

EIGHTY-NINE

"They triumphed over him by the blood of the
Lamb and by the word of their testimony ... "

Revelation 12:11a, NIV

Will you ever completely overcome your Anxiety Elephants? The answer is: YES, you will . . . it just takes time. You might want me to stop at YES, but you need to know up front, just as we have hashed over these past three months together, that time is a friend on this path. God's healing needs to infiltrate the places Anxiety Elephants have made their camp in for so long.

Today's scripture tells us *how* to overcome: by the blood of the Lamb and the word of our testimony.

Jesus did His part. He was the sacrificial lamb for our sin. Jesus paid a debt we would never be able to cover. He shed every drop of His blood on the cross for you and me. Now, it's your turn. There is someone out there who needs to hear your story. They need to hear how you are overcoming and how you are conquering anxiety. They need hope to know that if it can happen for another person, it can happen for them.

What I am challenging you to do is to help someone else. Share your testimony. Your story offers healing. If you see a friend struggling, let them know you understand and care. If you see someone post on social media, send a message of encouragement.

Think about it like this—where would you be if no one was willing to help and share with you? You can do this. God will help you. Now is your time to overcome.

THE NEXT SMALL STEP

Look for one person you can share with about how God has brought you healing. Ask God to give you the words others need to hear and open eyes to see who it is.

PRAYER

Thank You, Jesus, for doing Your part willingly for me. Help me to do my part and to share the testimony You have given me to lift others up.

JOURNAL

....

....

....

....

....

....

....

....

....

....

....

NINETY

"You, Lord, are my lamp; the Lord turns my darkness into light. With your help I can advance against a troop; with my God I can scale a wall. As for God, his way is perfect: The Lord's word is flawless; he shields all who take refuge in him."

2 Samuel 22:29-31, NIV

The Lord has just delivered David from his enemies, and David turns his words to a song of praise for all God did for him. As you turn to the last day of this book, my prayer is that you see God's hand delivering you from the hand of your enemy. For so long, Anxiety Elephants treated you much like David's enemies treated him. They looked to bring you physical harm. Their goal was to isolate you away from family, friends, and those who love and care for you. They tried extremely hard to make you believe God had left you and would not fulfill His promises because of all the past mistakes you have made. These Anxiety Elephants looked to leave you all alone, to dry up and not fulfill the calling God placed on you.

As God came through for David, look at what He has also done for you! His word has illuminated your path over these past ninety days. He has taken the dark places of lies and shined TRUTH through the faulty bars holding you back. He has provided you help and the freedom to use it by calling on His name or texting a friend. He has strengthened you in your faith to jump over any wall the enemy tries to push you back behind.

You have found safety in His presence. You have discovered healthy strategies to take care of yourself mentally. You have learned anxiety does not define you and struggles will never be wasted in God's plan for your life. You have been challenged to help others and to speak with boldness the testimony God has given you.

David's words at the end of this chapter are appropriate as we prepare to close this book: *"The Lord lives! Praise be to my Rock! Exalted be my God, the Rock, my Savior!"* 2 Samuel 22:47, NIV.

THE NEXT SMALL STEP

As you close this devotional, write out how you want to continue to grow in your relationship with God. Sign it, date it, and surrender your commitment to the Lord. Put it somewhere you can find it one year from now to look back on God's faithfulness.

PRAYER

Thank You, Father, for all the strategies I have learned and the weapons You have given me to stomp out Anxiety Elephants every day. You have given me everything I need to advance forward.

JOURNAL

....

....

....

....

....

....

....

....

....

CONCLUSION

The message has been somewhat similar over the past ninety days of insights into God's power, love, and mental strategy for your life. As each page was turned, you encountered particular themes at least once. God hears you, there is hope, you are never alone, and Anxiety Elephants can be defeated. You read multiple times about the importance of seeking help, taking your thoughts captive, accountability, changing old habits, prayer and worship.

Why would I include similar messages over and over?

Because reminders are needed! Anxiety Elephants have pushed their agenda into your mind and soul long enough. If they keep reciting the same messages of fear, shame, and judgment, we can use their plan against them and echo truth and hope daily. The new coping skills you have learned provide direction on how to daily care for and nourish your mind.

God has equipped you with everything you need for battle. We will continue to fight next to one another and for one another. Practice the next small steps and apply the new strategies etched into your blueprint for thinking and living.

You are ready. Keep fighting, friend.

ENDNOTES

1   "Anxiety Disorders." NAMI: National Alliance on Mental Illness.
    Accessed April 3, 2023. https://www.nami.org/About-Mental-
    Illness/Mental-Health-Conditions/Anxiety-Disorders.

2   "Definition of WORRY." Merriam-Webster Online Dictionary.
    Last modified November 28, 2022. https://www.merriam-
    webster.com/dictionary/worry.

3   "8849 Worry - Dictionary of Bible Themes - Bible Gateway."
    BibleGateway.com. Accessed April 3, 2023. https://
    www.biblegateway.com/resources/dictionary-of-bible-
    themes/8849-worry.

4   "Definition of CONSOLATION." Merriam-Webster Online
    Dictionary. Accessed June 20, 2023. https://www.merriam-
    webster.com/dictionary/consolation.

5   Porath, Teresa. "Public Speaking is No. 1 Fear of Many
    Americans." Midland Reporter-Telegram. Last modified
    March 27, 2018. https://www.mrt.com/news/health_and_
    wellness/article/Public-speaking-is-No-1-fear-of-many-
    Americans-12786022.php.

6   "EXPLAINING WHAT SIN IS TO CHILDREN – James 4:17."
    Walking with Yeshua (Jesus) - Bible Stories for Kids. Last
    modified February 16, 2020. https://wwyeshua.wordpress.
    com/2020/02/16/explaining-what-sin-is-to-children-
    james-417/.

ABOUT THE AUTHOR

 Caris Snider is the author of several books for children through adults on the subject of anxiety. She's the author of *Anxiety Elephants for Tweens, There's an Elephant on My Chest, Car Line Mom,* and more. She had undergone severe anxiety in her formative and adult years, and seeks to give readers biblical principles and coping exercises to work through their anxiety. Find out more about Caris at carissnider.com.